STORIES
TO
MAKE YOU
SMILE

STORIES TO MAKE YOU SMILE

EDITED BY
FANNY BLAKE

SIMON &
SCHUSTER

London · New York · Sydney · Toronto · New Delhi

First published in Great Britain by Simon & Schuster UK Ltd, 2021

Anthology Copyright © Read – The Reading Agency, 2021

The right of The Reading Agency to be identified as anthologist
of this work has been asserted in accordance with the
Copyright, Designs and Patents Act, 1988.

1 3 5 7 9 10 8 6 4 2

Simon & Schuster UK Ltd
1st Floor
222 Gray's Inn Road
London WC1X 8HB

Simon & Schuster Australia, Sydney
Simon & Schuster India, New Delhi

www.simonandschuster.co.uk
www.simonandschuster.com.au
www.simonandschuster.co.in

A CIP catalogue record for this book
is available from the British Library

ISBN: 978-1-3985-0578-0
eBook ISBN: 978-1-3985-0579-7

Typeset in Bembo by M Rules
Printed and bound by CPI Group (UK) Ltd, Croydon, CR0 4YY

Contents

About World Book Night

World Book Night is the annual celebration of books and reading on 23 April that brings people together for one reason – to inspire others to read more!

2021 marks the tenth anniversary of World Book Night. Since 2011, almost 3 million books have been gifted to new readers across the UK.

World Book Night is run by The Reading Agency, a national charity tackling life's big challenges through the proven power of reading. World Book Night 2021 is in partnership with Specsavers.

readingagency.org.uk
worldbooknight.org.uk
@readingagency
@WorldBookNight

The Reading Agency Ltd. Registered number: 3904882 (England & Wales)
Registered charity number: 1085443 (England & Wales)
Registered Office: Free Word Centre, 60 Farringdon Road, London, EC1R 3GA
The Reading Agency is supported using public funding by Arts Council England.

Supported using public funding by
**ARTS COUNCIL
ENGLAND**

The World Book Night 2021 Booklist

A Dutiful Boy by Mohsin Zaidi
Ask a Footballer by James Milner
Common People ed. by Kit de Waal
Elevation by Stephen King
Emma by Jane Austen
Faking Friends by Jane Fallon
Good Food for Bad Days by Jack Monroe
I Will Not Be Erased by gal-dem
Much Ado About Nothing by William Shakespeare
Pocket Book of Happiness
Reasons to Be Cheerful by Nina Stibbe
Simon vs. the Homo Sapiens Agenda by Becky Albertalli
Stories to Make You Smile ed. by Fanny Blake
Sunshine and Sweet Peas in Nightingale Square by Heidi Swain
Taking Up Space by Chelsea Kwakye and Ore Ogunbiyi
The Anxiety Survival Guide by Bridie Gallagher, Sue Knowles
and Phoebe McEwen, illustrated by Emmeline Pidgen
The Flatshare by Beth O'Leary
The Kindness Method by Shahroo Izadi
To Sir With Love by E.R. Braithwaite
Up in the Attic by Pam Ayres
We Are All Made of Molecules by Susin Nielsen
Where Are We Now? by Glenn Patterson

Find out about the books at **worldbooknight.org**

Continue your reading journey

The Reading Agency is here to help keep you and your family reading:

Challenge yourself to complete six reads by taking part in Reading Ahead at your local library, college or workplace
readingahead.org.uk

Join Reading Groups for Everyone to find a reading group and discover new books
readinggroups.org.uk

Read with your family as part of the Summer Reading Challenge at your local library and online
summerreadingchallenge.org.uk

Discover Quick Reads, short books by best-selling authors
readingagency.org.uk/quickreads

For more information, please visit our website:
readingagency.org.uk

Keeping readers focused since 1984

Something to smile about

Specsavers

Behind My Fat Back

by Jenny Éclair

This changing room has two mirrors spitefully positioned to simultaneously reflect one's bulges both front and back. I don't normally see my rear view and I am slightly bemused by the number of creases in the flesh under my bra strap. Back fat is pointless really, we're not camels, camels store fat in their humps, so they can cross the desert without stopping off for a cheeseburger . . . or whatever camels eat?

I am a large white woman, there is something rather tripe-like about my skin tones and judging by my reflection I am probably two stone overweight. This is why I am sitting in the changing room of 'Angela Young's Bridal and Special Occasion Fashion Emporium' (Prom Dresses and Formal Hire also Available), waiting for the assistant to bring me something I might feasibly be able to get both arms into, preferably without any Swarovski beading.

Apparently I'd been optimistic asking for a size sixteen. Inevitably I'd got stuck and then panicked trying to get the thing off. Consequently there is a tiny rip under the arm of a fuchsia lace bolero, which we shan't mention.

'I'll bring the eighteen and the, um ...' – she couldn't say 'size twenty' out loud – '... the next size up from that, just to be on the safe side.' That was ten minutes ago.

While I wait, I perch in the corner of this curtained-off torture chamber on a fragile gilded chair, half expecting the thing to collapse under me. When one is my size, one learns to avoid flimsy furniture. Wicker chairs and ancient deckchairs basically scream public humiliation and a cracked coccyx.

No doubt the seating at the wedding will be similarly insubstantial, light and stackable, the usual arrangement for a marquee-style service. Not that I'm religious. I couldn't care less where they get married. What I do like, however, is the sturdiness of an old-fashioned wooden church pew.

I'm here under extreme duress and strict instruction. My sister, aka 'the Mother of the Bride', said this was the place to come. It has chandeliers and thick cream carpets. I nearly took my shoes off at the door. If I had, no doubt they'd have hidden them. This is a strictly heels-only establishment and a pair of size-seven lace-ups with orthotic inserts in an extra-wide fitting would no doubt be seen as a blight.

This is a novel experience for me; I normally buy my clothes from the supermarket. I dress mostly in navy even though it shows up the dog hairs, only it doesn't at the moment because I am between dogs. Oh God, if I think about Pepsi, I might cry. Mind you, if I think about buying an outfit for this stupid wedding, I might cry.

I genuinely don't understand why people are still going

through this ridiculous charade when heterosexual couples can finally opt for a no-nonsense civil partnership.

But then, as I am constantly reminded, I wouldn't understand because I have never been married, just as I can't possibly understand what it's like to have children because I have never given birth.

Women like me – single, barren and ageing – are considered emotionally neutered. We just wouldn't 'understand'.

Apparently my role as aunt and godmother of the bride is to fade gracefully into the background. My hat should be small and quiet and obviously I mustn't wear white or black or red. I asked my sister Veronica why I couldn't wear red. I understand the black and white rules, the bride wears white and black belongs to funerals or bondage clubs (oh, the temptation to go for black leather) – but red, why not red? Veronica said, and I quote, 'Because wearing red is a sign of madness at your age and anyway you have a tendency to a flushed cheek and wearing red just makes you look like you've been on the sherry since breakfast.'

Ah, yes, that's another thing, alcohol. Apparently I should stick to two small glasses of champagne, as any more inflames my sinuses and I start to make snoring noises when I breathe. I can't help it . . . it drives Veronica mad. 'It sounds like you're bored when you're talking to people.' Yes . . . well.

My sister is micro-managing this wedding despite the fact that Madeline has insisted on hiring a professional wedding planner called Summer who looks like she was born with a migraine and wears beige nail varnish. Seriously, I think some of these girls watch far too much American TV. What's wrong with a registry office and a pork pie in the pub? After all, there are no money-back guarantees with marriages. You can spend fifty grand on a white silk tent, an iced-swan vodka luge and a chocolate fountain, but if it all goes tits-up in six months' time, Veronica and Mike won't get a penny back. It will all have been for nothing.

When I think of all the wedding gifts I've bought people for marriages that haven't survived, I visualize them on a conveyor belt, an entire *Generation Game*'s worth of goodies: egg coddlers, novelty chess sets, an Indonesian back scratcher, silver-plated cocktail shaker . . . and for what?

I genuinely think that if a marriage crumbles before the guarantees are up on a wedding gift, then that gift should be returned to sender, preferably with a note of abject apology: 'Sorry we made you slog out to the arse-end of Buckinghamshire and fork out for train tickets, taxis and a night in a hideous bed and breakfast with melamine wardrobes and nylon curtains, not to mention the cost of a new outfit, hat and pair of pinchy shoes, just so you could stand in a field and watch me and someone you wouldn't recognize in a line-up of IT consultants with fashionable beards exchange vows that neither of us intended to keep for more than three and a half months. Anyway, here's your fire pit back, we only used it once.'

I went off-piste for Madeline. She sent out this gift list from Peter Jones. I thought, *Sod that,* and I bought her a ventriloquist's dummy from a little place in Brighton.

Veronica was furious when I told her, she kept saying, 'But she wanted a gravy boat and six Royal Doulton Pacific porcelain pasta bowls.' Well, if she wants them so much, then she and Jack or Josh or Joe can buy them themselves.

Madeline will make a beautiful, if emaciated, bride. That's another thing about weddings, why does everyone have to lose half their body weight before the big day? I remember when Veronica got married, she was an utter cow for six months before she squeezed herself into that gown. Poor Mike, I'm surprised he recognized her coming down the aisle, she could have been an entirely different woman, she was a stone thinner and her hair was two shades darker – she looked like the ghost of Morticia Addams. Honestly, she was so weak, I thought my dad would have to give her a fireman's lift all the way down the aisle. She'd lived on nothing but Silk Cut and celery for six months and consequently her breath was foul. Seriously, when the vicar said, 'You may now kiss the bride,' I swear Mike recoiled.

I was only allowed to be her bridesmaid on the proviso that I too lost weight. Of course, this was thirty years ago, when I was in my mid-twenties. Veronica had the dress made for my target size and it was touch and go for weeks before the actual ceremony. Fortunately, I got a nasty case of quinsy a fortnight before the big day and, as luck would have it, a life-threatening peritonsillar abscess achieved the desired effect. My mother and Veronica cheered when the zip went all the way up without having to use pliers.

I cut the dress up a few months later, made a lampshade for

the spare bedroom. There was quite a lot of fabric left over. I couldn't burn it because it was synthetic and I was worried about the fumes, and I couldn't take it down to the charity shop because it had this big lampshade-shaped hole in it, so I buried it in the garden. It felt like I was getting rid of a body. I have refused to diet ever since.

My only regret about not getting married is that I never got to inflict anything in peach sateen on anyone else. When I eventually admitted to Veronica that I'd got rid of the dress, she said, 'I wish I hadn't bothered asking you, I could have had two normal-sized bridesmaids out of the same amount of fabric and still had enough left over for a little flower girl.'

She can be quite cutting, can Veronica. Madeline is twenty-nine, which is apparently peak bride age. Veronica said, 'She wants to get that ring on her finger before she's thirty because no one wants to get lumbered with the left-overs.' Personally I can't see what's wrong with left-overs? Let's face it, there's nothing more delicious for breakfast than last night's takeaway curry.

I am getting rather cold now, so I put my cardigan on over my 'seen better days' underwear and I reach into my tote bag for a prawn sandwich that I just so happen to have upon my person. Not being a camel, I refuse to set out on an arduous shopping trek without sustenance. A prawn falls out and lands on the crotch of my pants but I scoop it up and eat it anyway. It's a very good sandwich, lots of tangy Marie Rose sauce. I think the assistant has forgotten me, such is the invisibility of middle age.

Suddenly I am aware of raised voices on the shop floor: a bride sobbing hysterically over some terrible Michael Bublé track. In between sobs, she is wailing that she hates her dress, the bodice makes her look fat, she doesn't like the neckline and she doesn't fucking want to get married to 'that twat' anyway.

I have to stifle a laugh, because obviously this is no laughing matter.

'Call me Angie', the proprietor of Angela Young's Bridal and Special Occasion Fashion Emporium, can be heard to offer our jittery bride a Buck's Fizz and some tedious platitudes about pre-wedding nerves, while an older woman who is obviously the bride's mother tells her to 'bloody snap out of it'.

It's Veronica! I recognized her voice as soon as she said 'bloody'. We are both originally from the North but she's done her best to disguise it over the years. Mike is very Home Counties, but the Lancashire in Veronica comes out when she's mad. I freeze on my tiny gilt chair, as my sister launches into a tirade befitting a fishwife. 'Now, listen here, young lady, you're getting married whether you like it or not. I've got a down payment on that marquee and the cake alone cost £750. Do you want to end up fat and lonely and on the shelf like your Aunty Gina, covered in dog hairs and living in a pebbledash bungalow? Hmm? Is that what you want? Talking to yourself because you've got no one else to talk to. Everyone feeling sorry for you.'

'Ooh, no, you don't want that,' says Call Me Angie. 'Not

when you've got a lovely Duchess ivory silk frock with three thousand individually stitched seed pearls ready to waft you up that aisle in three days' time.'

I sit. I sit very calmly and wait for my sister and my niece to leave the shop, then I drop my sandwich wrapper on the floor of the changing room, get dressed and go home to my pebbledash bungalow.

It is ten past five by the time I get indoors; by a quarter to six I have booked an all-inclusive ten-day holiday to Morocco. I leave on Saturday. The seat will be small and uncomfortable but I won't care. I will be 35,000 feet in the air wearing jogging bottoms and Velcro shoes and I shall drink as much champagne as I like.

Oh, and I'll tell you another thing. I'm keeping that ventriloquist's dummy.

Jenny Éclair is the *Sunday Times* top-ten bestselling author of the critically acclaimed novels *Camberwell Beauty*, *Having a Lovely Time*, *Life, Death and Vanilla Slices* and *Inheritance*, as well as the Richard & Judy bestseller, *Moving*, and the short-story collection, *Listening In*. Her most recent non-fiction book, *Older and Wider: A Survivor's Guide to the Menopause*, was published in 2020.

One of the UK's most popular writer/performers, she was the first woman to win the prestigious Perrier Award and has many TV and radio credits to her name. She lives in south-east London and co-hosts the popular podcast 'Older and Wider'.

Schooled

by Mark Watson

'Now, in this company we like to see ourselves as people who do things a little differently. People who can adapt to the unexpected, think on their feet, deal with new situations. As we've had to do quite a bit today, what with everything that's happened! And I do apologize again for all that ... for the mix-ups, for the interruptions.'

'Oh, that's fine,' says Lloyd.

He doesn't have any choice. It's true that the interview has been a complete shambles, but he can't afford to vocalize his bewilderment at how badly things have been run. This is the horrible position that it puts you into, job-seeking: somewhere between a polite visitor, an appreciative tourist and a supplicant. Even when you see incompetence around you, even when it is almost embarrassingly clear that you would add value to the set-up – because almost *anyone* would, because quite honestly a badger in a suit would – you still have to feign admiration and respect. When the person interviewing you makes spelling errors in the introductory email, when the firm gets the time wrong and double-books you: however amateurish the team and their actions, you still have to act as if it would be a privilege to join their ranks. Because you are separated from them by one of the starkest measurements that can divide people. They have a job and you do not.

You are here dipping your little fishing net into a fast-flowing river, trying to grab at something which the person on the other side of the table already possesses. You cannot help feeling that this must be because they have done something right which you did wrong. On some level that has to be true.

So Lloyd has to be polite about the frankly atrocious organization of this day so far: the late start, the leak in the ceiling which was bizarrely never acknowledged, the guy *barging in to get a signature for a bloody pizza*, for God's sake. And now he's going to have to play along with whatever stupid scenario they're going to finish this ordeal with. He's heard 'we like to do things differently' from these kinds of people before. In fact, he's struggling to think of a firm that *doesn't* believe it's doing things differently. It's one of the few things all businesses have in common.

'So with that in mind . . .' says the interviewer. A tall guy, handsome, good teeth. Younger than Lloyd himself, which always stings. Makes it feel like they're not just ahead of you in the race of life, but have actually lapped you. The counsellor he saw last year was on about not seeing everything like that, like a race. Getting out of that mental pattern, 'rejecting the narrative'. But then the free sessions ran out, before she had told Lloyd how he was meant to do that.

'Yes?' says Lloyd. The interviewer is really enjoying this. He almost certainly devised it himself – this demeaning exercise, whatever it's going to be. Or he stole it from some business book. Or more likely he read an extract from the business book on an Instagram story and stole it from *that*.

'What I'm going to ask you to do,' says the interviewer, 'is stand up and pull your trousers down. What do you say to that?'

Stacey's two-way radio buzzes, but she ignores it and cradles the coffee in its throwaway cup. She really just wanted it for the feeling of holding a hot drink; she doubts she'll drink it. The machine wheezed and moaned as she pressed the buttons; the liquid dribbled out with what looked a painful effort. They don't have a nice coffee machine here like in their home office, let alone an actual catering team, because this – of course – is not a real workspace. It isn't a real *anything*. It's just a crudely constructed backdrop for a mean trick, as usual. Stacey's tired of tricks and stunts being her main job in life; of her reality being composed of things which aren't real. That's why it ends today. That's why she has already sown the seeds of her own sacking.

The radio goes again and, at the same time, the phone thrums gently with a text. There's no point messing about with these little radios when phones exist. They're leftovers from a different age, like the clipboards and notepads people also insist on carrying around. Stacey doesn't even check the phone. She already knows what's happening down the corridor, and she hasn't got the heart to witness it in person, even though this is the final time she'll have to do it.

The infantile 'trousers down' thing is the final cue. As soon as the victim has responded with bafflement, horror, confusion – maybe even done the humiliating thing he's been asked to, such is his exhaustion by this stage – ticker-tape will come from hidden vents in the walls, a banner will be unfurled, music will play. The 'interviewer' will remove his fake glasses, break into a broad, telegenic grin, extend his hand in consolation and utter the popular catchphrase: 'You have just been schooled!' He will reveal himself not to have been a recruitment officer for an IT startup at all, but Iain Trainor – 'The Train', as he wearyingly signs off on his social media, as his fans even more wearyingly insist on calling him when they send their weird little gifts to the set. He will explain that he, Iain Trainor, the king of televised practical jokes, has struck yet again. There never was a job. There never was a company looking to hire someone like Lloyd. All this – the week-long wait, the botched logistics and the catalogue of misfortunes that have befallen the interview day itself – all this has been for the entertainment of a few hundred thousand strangers, and for the continuation of The Train's impressive career momentum.

And Lloyd, who has unknowingly already signed paper-work to allow this footage to be used: well, Lloyd will have to be a *good sport* about it, clap himself on the forehead in self-mockery, record a piece to camera where he says he abso-lutely wants the ground to open up and swallow him, he can't believe it, he did think something was weird here but he never imagined he was actually talking to The Train. His friends are going to take the piss so bad! He's going to hide under the sofa when this goes on the TV! All these soundbites and whatever else the director reads off his stupid clipboard. Then they'll take Lloyd to the green room and give him a beer; Iain Trainor will say, 'Nice one, mate. No harm done!' without looking up from his phone and then disappear off with his manager and PA. They'll get Lloyd a car home and forget about him, begin working on the next episode. And in the morning, Lloyd, of course, will still not have a job, or the prospect of one.

When it began a couple of years ago, Stacey wasn't merely grateful for the job, the income and the status it provided; she actively enjoyed it. The show, in its infancy, was a gentler proposition, almost joyful in its silliness – even for the casualties of its pranks. Somebody would repeatedly receive takeaways they hadn't ordered, or workmen would show up at their house claiming to have a commission to dig an outdoor swimming pool. A headmaster's end-of-year address would be interrupted by an apparent lunatic walking a goat right into the school hall (this was in the pilot episode, in fact, and it was what gave rise to the eventual name of the series). The stunts were harmless, often imaginative; the crew would laugh a lot as they unfolded, would text photos to their friends. There was a sense of pride in the work, frivolous as it undoubtedly was. Iain Trainor hadn't yet undergone the ego-inflation that a TV success and its accoutrements can pipe into the veins. At that point Stacey was happy to sign on for three more series. Everyone was.

But the tone has changed, there's no mistaking it. There are many competing shows in this genre now, and that climate of competition has forced everyone to 'raise the stakes', as the director put it recently. In this environment, what 'raising the stakes' means is, in human terms, being meaner, causing actual suffering rather than simply chagrin and embarrassment. People receiving letters that accuse them of involvement in crimes they couldn't have committed; fake court summonses; people being tailed by mysterious cars or getting unexplained knocks on the door at night. And, increasingly, the victims being found not by nomination from friends and family – that got too risky, it was too easy for them to blab – but by a semi-legal trawl of databases. They'd entered a competition online, perhaps, or got free tickets to recordings in the past. Stacey knows this, because part of her job title is 'researcher'. It was Stacey who was charged with digging Lloyd's name up from some online scrapyard, establishing that he had been out of work for some months, would be delighted even to get to interview stage. When she saw him for the first time during the hidden-camera record day, saw his battle-weary face and ill-fitting suit and thought about what was going to happen to him, she knew she was done with this.

She had mentally walked away from the show by the time she got off the underground that night. The plan that followed took a little longer to form.

'Nice one, mate,' says The Train. 'No harm done, eh!'

His manager, in a new and conspicuously expensive fake

fur coat, totters behind him with a black Armani carrier bag, containing a two-piece suit, over her arm. Iain Trainor is off to a student union this evening, where he is getting paid four thousand pounds for an 'appearance'. This entails about ten minutes on stage answering pre-agreed questions from whichever nervy undergrad has landed the job of hosting, followed by a stint of selfie-posing and then the best bit: an exit, via the back of the building, to a Mercedes whose engine has not stopped running since he was dropped off.

Stacey knows about the fee because on one of the rare occasions he got drunk with the crew members, he bragged about it at some length. She also knows his planned movements for tonight, but that information was gained with more difficulty and stealth. After the brief, lucrative trip to the student union, the Mercedes will take him back to the house he recently bought, in west London: an eighty-minute trip, all paid for by the people who hired him to appear. He will be home, Stacey has calculated, by about half past eleven. It doesn't matter if he's a little later than that. It will all be waiting for him.

Iain Trainor will see it, in fact, before he even gets out of the vehicle. He'll sense something is up as soon as he gets on to the normally quiet street. A crowd of people late at night. Curiosity turning to cold fear as it becomes obvious that number 62 is the focus of their attention. And then, as he snaps open the door, gets his own stuff out of the boot – not waiting, as he usually would, for it to be handed to him – the redoubling of that fear by everything he sees.

Smoke cascading out of upstairs windows. Fire extinguishers being sprayed, firemen in uniform assembling, broken glass on the floor, neighbours emerging to watch. Sirens, raised voices, mobile phones raised and held as tiny TV cameras. The property being trampled, damaged, full of strangers, his stuff being manhandled, all hands on deck to spare him the worst of the disaster.

It's taken Stacey a week to organize; it wouldn't have been possible if she didn't have a friend who ran a drama troupe, and if she hadn't been prepared to throw a bit of money at this petty project, and most of all – of course – if she hadn't learned a lot about sourcing things like smoke machines and prop explosives over the past couple of years. Perhaps the job hasn't been such a waste of time after all.

She looks at Ian, 'The Train', making his oblivious way towards his car – a handshake for the more senior production staff, a brief flirty word for his favourite make-up girl – and forces back a smile. She sees herself – a few hours from now – taking a video of the carnage at 62 Grosvenor Gardens, ghosting away before he can comprehend what's been done to him, and how. A video archived for her own satisfaction, but not exclusively hers. Lloyd will be surprised by a WhatsApp message late at night. *I thought you might like to see that someone else got 'schooled' today*, she might write. *No harm done!*

Mark Watson is the acclaimed author of nine books, most recently *Contacts*, *The Place that Didn't Exist*, *Hotel Alpha* and *The Knot*, which have been published in twelve languages. He is also a stand-up comedian and has won numerous awards in Britain and Australia. He regularly appears on TV, has had his own cult Radio 4 series and been named the Edinburgh Festival's highest achiever of the decade by *The Times*. He lives in north London.

The First Birthday Party

by Veronica Henry

There were half a dozen of them: six little tyrants in their highchairs round the table. None of them had any idea why they'd been rudely awoken from their afternoon nap to be brought here. Of course they didn't: apart from the birthday boy they were all just under twelve months old, the offspring of the new best friends I'd met at Mother and Toddlers or, as we secretly liked to call it, the Post-Natal Depression Club.

We were all still slightly shell-shocked by our new lives and our new roles. We were still tentative and uncertain with each other, just as we were tentative and uncertain of ourselves. Each week we gathered in a circle on the floor of the medical centre, crusted in chewed rusk, holding our bandy-legged offspring aloft, none of them quite on the move yet but all champing at the bit to make a break for freedom.

We discussed sleep – or lack of it. Sore boobs, saggy tummies, sex – or lack of it. The horror and the joy of it all bonded us quickly, with sympathetic smiles, nods of agreement and a touch on the shoulder if one of us became tearful.

was the mum I was most drawn to, but she was also the
…n I was most worried about. She was always exhausted
…nd was obviously struggling with a child who hardly slept.
But when she laughed, I caught a glimpse of her spirit and
warmth. Somehow, though, there was never time to bond.
We always had to race home, conscious of teatime and bath-
time and bedtime, our new regime.

Dylan was the eldest of the group so I drew the short
straw and was the first to hold a birthday party. As a single
mum, I had a lot to prove. I was up at six, cutting bread for
sandwiches into star shapes, eager to impress. The house
looked as if a bomb had hit it. I rushed around, picking up
clothes and toys and hoping there wasn't a stray dirty nappy
lurking anywhere, the ultimate crime. By lunchtime, order
was restored. My tiny little home was shabby and worn but
clean and welcoming. You can do this, I told myself, dressing
Dylan in a fresh pair of jeans and a yellow polo shirt, kissing
him over and over again. One year old!

At two, the guests arrived and shiny parcels were placed in
a pile on the kitchen table. My heart sank slightly, knowing
Dylan didn't really need any more stuff. I was already sweat-
ing at the thought of finding time to write them thank-you
notes. The smallest tasks seemed impossible these days.

The mothers all hovered behind the highchairs like dutiful
footmen, curating their children's plates. A cube of cheese
and a carrot stick for the health-conscious; crisps and ham
sandwiches for those who didn't give a fig for the state of
their child's kidneys. Anything that met with disapproval

got dropped on the floor: soon it was awash with halves of green grape and chunks of cucumber. I'd spent hours slicing them up!

As the troughs of their pelican bibs filled with crumbs, I brought in plates of Pink Panther wafers, Jammie Dodgers and chocolate fingers. There was a real party atmosphere now: in the background, the cassette player wheezed jolly tunes over and over: 'Miss Polly Had a Dolly', 'I Went to the Animal Fair', 'The Wheels on the Bloody Bus'.

I looked around at my new friends. The dark circles under their eyes. The unbrushed hair. The baggy sweatshirts over the jeans. The air of slight desperation, but also the love in their eyes as they wiped tiny fingers with a damp flannel or brushed a lock of hair across a sweaty forehead. As the children grew tired of eating, we all clawed at the remains of the food casually, unable to resist the synthetic lure.

As the hands of the clock dragged themselves round, I made an executive decision. We deserved a treat too – our grown-up equivalent of party food.

'Does anyone fancy a glass of wine?'

Everyone looked startled. They all looked at each other, unsure. One or two darted me a look of faux disapproval, and suddenly I felt flooded with shame. Obviously, as a single mum, my morals and standards were low. Then Suki said, 'Why the hell not? We deserve it, don't we?' I flashed her a grateful glance, my gut feeling about her confirmed.

I pulled a bottle of Lambrusco out of the fridge and filled up the paper cups. Everyone started to relax. I changed the cassette to the latest dance anthems and the tunes blared out to smiles of recognition as we all remembered our pre-baby nights out in discos and nightclubs. We plucked our darlings out of their chairs and danced around the room together. For a while we were the women we'd once been, carefree on the dancefloor. The babies loved it as their mothers twirled, holding them aloft, and by some miracle there was no projectile vomiting. This was our moment to feel free, and the groove was definitely in all of our hearts.

And then 'Ride on Time' by Black Box came on and Suki took the centre of the room. We all melted away as she began to dance, and by the fluidity of her moves we began to realize she must be a professional. We rarely talked about our former lives, or who we had been, or what we had done, but here she was, spinning faster and faster, her braids flying, supple and sinuous and mesmerizing. She wasn't showing off, she was losing herself in what she loved. We all applauded as the song came to an end, and she bowed, laughing, breathless, but more alive than we'd ever seen her.

The guests left. Each of my friends gave me a hug, their breath sweet with Lambrusco and Pink Panthers. Somehow the afternoon had broken the ice between us.

Suki was the last to leave. She threw her arms around my neck and whispered in my ear: 'Is it very hard? Being a single mum?'

I looked at her, startled. 'I'm not sure it's any harder than being a married one. Why?'

'I want to go back to work. I've been offered an amazing

part in a show. But my husband ...' She gulped, obviously struggling to hold back the tears. 'My husband says a good mother should always put her child first.'

I put my arm around her. 'Not at the expense of yourself,' I told her firmly. 'Being a good mum means being the best version of you.'

She looked up at me. Her eyes were glassy, but there was determination in them. 'I think I'm going to leave him,' she said. 'You've shown me it can be done. This was the best party ever.'

I hesitated. 'That's a big decision.' I didn't want to be responsible for breaking up a relationship, but I'd seen the strain she was under. 'But I'm always here. I've got a spare room if you need it ...'

Twenty-nine years later I'm rushing around like a dervish again, the same pre-party sense of panic driving me as I wonder what I've forgotten. It's a different kitchen, a different house, a different menu, but my motive is the same: to make this a wonderful party. A landmark celebration for the son I love so much: Dylan is thirty years old today. His brother and sisters will be here, and his legion of friends. And it won't start until late. No one cool, apparently, turns up to a party before ten o'clock. I hope that I can stay the course; that I won't droop before midnight.

The invitations have gone out, photocopies of a photo of him from that first birthday, waving a chocolate finger around in his highchair, his face smothered. I've downloaded a playlist of the same dance tunes, remembering how he used to sing along to them in the car, his own toddler interpretation of the words making me laugh. The 1990s are back in again, so it's a cool theme for the party, and the guests start to arrive in their neon rave gear and Nirvana plaid brandishing glow sticks.

I've made it a modern-day replica of his very first party. There are sausages, of course, because a birthday party is nothing without sausages, but they are free-range and organic and cooked on the barbecue by Ben, the single dad I met on a Cornish beach the summer Dylan was four. Ben had two kids, a boy and a girl, and we went on to have two more girls between us. It's been glorious chaos.

And some of the guests are the same. Some of those sleep-deprived mums stayed the course, and have come along with their offspring, Dylan's childhood coterie. His partners in crime, mostly towering over me, pulling me into their big bear hugs. They have beards and tattoos and smell of after-shave and make me feel safe.

And at half ten, Suki arrives, and there's a ripple of recognition from everyone at the party. She's in a skin-tight tuxedo in bright pink, her millions of braids tied on top of her head. As Dylan sees her, he runs towards her and takes her hand, leading her to the middle of the room. Someone flips the playlist and the familiar notes of 'Sex Bomb' pound out as they take the floor.

The two of them are magnificent together. Not a foot-step out of place. It's a joy to watch. And my heart fills with pride. She's a household name, my darling friend, a judge on *Tango Foxtrot*, the hugely popular dance show. And Dylan is one of the professional dancers who partner the celebrities who take part. The most popular one, I'm proud to say. The one everyone wants to be paired with. He's an icon. A role model. And a bloody good dancer.

It was Suki who spotted his talent when Dylan was tiny and encouraged him. She lived with us for three years when she left her husband. We supported each other as we went on to live out our dreams, all crushed up in my little house that obligingly stretched out its walls to keep us in its embrace. She took the part in the show she'd been offered, and somehow we muddled through. We shared a nanny between us so I was able to go back to work too, as head of HR for a record company. It was the happiest household, filled with music and laughter and dancing. We shared the cooking and the cleaning and when Suki made enough money to be able to stand on her own two feet and move out to a place of her own, I cried for nearly a week.

But tonight I laugh and clap as Suki and Dylan finish their dance to uproarious applause. Suki winds her way over to me through the guests and hands me a bottle out of her handbag. The label looks familiar.

'Remember that Lambrusco you gave us? At Dylan's first birthday?' she says. 'I've never been so grateful for a glass of wine. You were a bloody legend. And imagine if you hadn't? We wouldn't be here now.'

Moments later I chink glasses with her, celebrating the

solidarity that has seen us through the ups and downs of motherhood and our determination to follow our dreams.

'Pink Panther?' I ask, proffering a plateful. We sit on the kitchen island with our arms around each other, drinking our wine, nibbling the sweet, dusty wafers and swinging our legs to the beat, happy in the knowledge that we are the very best version of ourselves we could possibly be, thanks to a moment of impulse that changed our lives. And a glass of Lambrusco.

Veronica Henry has written twenty-one bestselling novels, including *A Night on the Orient Express* and the *Beach Hut* series. She lives on the coast in North Devon and loves swimming in the sea and Negronis – though never together. Her latest book, *A Day at the Beach Hut,* is a collection of short stories and recipes and is due out in summer 2021.

Purpose

by Eva Verde

Polly understands why the checking and the box ticking is important. Before they put you on the pills, you've got to show a bit of willing. Especially when – according to her rude new doctor – all Polly Jessen really needs is company.

'We're social creatures at heart, Ms Jessen – those pesky lockdowns haven't helped matters . . . And you live alone, too? When, may I ask, was the last time you had a proper chat with someone?'

Polly thinks, refusing to reveal that it was likely the Amazon man, the witty bit of back and forth over whether she was old enough to sign for her deal-of-the-day 70cl Gordon's Gin delivery – which, on thinking, *was* last week. Six days ago, at least. Perhaps the doctor had a point.

'You turned fifty, last month, I see. We'll get you in for bloods, too. I suggest eye and hearing tests, when you can arrange them, but let's check weight and urine, while you're here . . .'

Bloods arranged. A joyful smear test booked. A grudging agreement to at least try 'getting active'. And a promise to attend Community Conversations, a Thursday morning social club, at the civic centre. What a load of . . .

But it must be so. Thursday's trip to the centre comes too fast for Polly. She lurks at the back of the hall, hopeful of claiming a distant seat until the group leader encourages her forward. Polly shuffles a few rows closer. It's all she'll compromise. Besides, she's only here to tick a box, only wants to sleep. Those night-time sounds from the flat below don't help. The woman's cry, drifting through the floorboards, keeps Polly wide awake in memory of her own failures – and brings it all home, so raw, so true. How helpless and paining it can feel, to be alone, when it's not your choice.

A side door opens, and in come more joiners, a mother and child this time, choosing the next chair but one to Polly. Distance is still preferred by most, the nightmares of those old daily pandemic updates never far away. The leader smiles, first at the buggy, then at the woman pushing it, now nervously freeing her child of the hat and gloves the central heating has fast made redundant. Groping through her bag with growing panic, the woman at last pulls her mobile free, squinting at the screen before pushing the volume into silence. With the bag safely between her feet, she glances left, towards Polly.

Ma, even with her eyes, recognizes the wide, owl-like face, knows it's Judgy Jessen from upstairs. Always red and put-out-looking. And how anyone can be judgy in footwear like that, Ma'll never know. Flip-flops, even in February.

Neighbours for five months, sharing even fewer words, yet Ma's forever been aware of the presence upstairs – never more so than when they first moved in; the curtain twitching as she'd lugged in her boxes and bedding. The whole estate were nosy replicas, as well, but at the same time cultivated distance, ignoring Ma and Skye, like they were less than air. Most had lived in the low-rise flats since their mid-60s construction. Being situated on the arse-end of nowhere didn't help, either. New people, *young people*, were rare sightings. And jarring.

Still, a smile for Skye, an exchange of basic pleasantries with Ma might be nice, might make a healthy, modern change. But Ma doesn't need them. She'd not swap her troubles to be a dry old crust like her neighbours, for all the money in the world.

It's the child Polly Jessen recognizes first. The girl downstairs – Skye, she thinks. Her little legs in white wool tights remind Polly of the times she took small daughters and fat baby legs for granted. Before they grew long and leggy and distant. Then flew away, for good.

The women, aware of each other, but used to feigning indifference, face forwards, focusing on the leader's monologue, which is odd, considering everyone's surely here for the conversation. But for the epic speech and the sound of Skye quietly turning the pages of her book, the room is quiet – until, that is, someone slips low-key wind.

Ma questions if she's even really heard it, more a squeak than anything else, but the sudden creeping stench leaves her certain.

'Ma?' Skye squishes her nose into a cheeky grimace. 'It wasn't me, Ma.'

Another squeak. Just to her left. An intake of breath, stifled laughter. The Jessen woman, shaking like a set jelly with a hand over her mouth to stop the infectious piglet-like snorts that Ma, beyond such childishness, catches anyway. The leader pauses and as Ma senses disapproval her laughter fades, her face growing hot, cursing all the while why she's here in the first place. But being here makes Ma a good mum, shows that Skye's thriving – and they don't need help. This, ToddlerCircle, Happy-Hands and AfterCare all keep the social worker and the health visitor making their little ticks in Skye's growth development booklet so that one day there won't be any more watch, watch, bloody watching.

A new disruption comes from Polly Jessen as she stands up. One Ma can't help but admire. Walking out, Polly mutters, 'This tosh ain't for me.'

Skye's buggy whizzes across the pavement as Ma tries beating the imminent rain, swerving expertly around the waterfalling litter from a full-up bin. It doesn't occur to Ma that she might be a natural in a car, too. The idea of learning to drive is unfathomable, like visiting the moon, and besides, how could she ever fully trust her eyes when they can change at the change of a mood? Once, the little black specks were a rarity, but lately it's like they've made a home in Ma's head, multiplying in tune with her worries.

The best thing Ma does, these days, is to turn any worry into something for Skye; one small thing so the day is never completely black, that keeps their small world turning free from interference. The dreaded clubs Skye somehow loves.

The library. A bus ride. Now, it's an iced bun on the way home, that the bread man always gives to Skye for free since Ma's pride melted enough to just say, thank you.

On her second cuppa, Polly sits in the bakery window, her cream horn untouched. And it surprises Polly, as much as it surprises Ma, when Skye's deft wheels slow beside her table to say hello. Leaning as far forwards as the buggy straps allow, Skye's finger dives first into the cream horn, then her small waiting mouth.

'Skye!'

Polly Jessen laughs for the second time this morning; the second time in far too long. Pushing her plate towards Skye, she offers Ma a seat.

'Why d'you wear them?' Ma, who has become Malorie, asks, after a bit, now with her own cup of tea. 'The flip-flops?'

'Don't like feeling trapped, is all.' Polly shifts uncomfortably. 'And I'm too antisocial to stay anywhere long enough for frostbite.'

'I've never been much of a talker.' Ma squeezes her girl, now in her lap, who Ma will never let know how it feels when nobody listens. Skye wriggles free, too curious for cuddles. 'But it's been nice, saying hello properly.'

'Bonding over blow-offs.' Polly tries a smile, but her eyes won't quite let her. 'You take care, Malorie.' Polly pushes Skye's nose. 'And you, Wotsit.'

Ma, used to relying on her other senses, feels sorrow in the spiky, childish humour, noting the same stiff distance in Polly that Ma wears, too, even as she pays the bill with a note, rather than working out change.

Climbing into her buggy, Skye's book slips to the floor with a splat. Picking it up, Polly hands the book back. 'You'll be wanting Ma to read that later.'

'I read to Ma. 'Cos she—'

But a flustered Ma returns, shushing Skye, who just won't have it.

'Walk home with us, Polly. Pleeease.'

Other than her GP's professional yet sterile contact yesterday, holding Skye's hand along the pavement is Polly's first proper physical connection in longer than she cares to remember. Warm purpose, all too briefly over as Polly pulls Ma quickly from the road, saving her from screeching tyres and the angry, terrified shouts of the man behind the wheel, his burnt-out brakes the pungent proof of how close Ma comes to forever blacking out.

Panicked and scared, but oh so grateful, Ma reaches for Skye. Then, it's like she conjured them herself, as tiny black dots swarm across her vision, swallowing the wheels and shouts and chaos. Swallowing everything.

Warmth, twice this morning. But Skye on her lap creates unbearable nostalgia for her own grown girl, who lives as far from Polly as she can. But it also feels good, having something to do. She'll keep watch for now, an eye on Skye while Ma's checked over. And Polly always did like having someone to look after.

'You must think I'm the crappiest mother on earth.' Waiting in the busy A&E, Ma clears her throat as the dark thoughts rush together again, a haze of buzzing, awkward movement that she blinks clear, to watch her girl, so happy on that strange woman's lap. Skye's tongue pokes from her mouth like the tip of a thumb as she doodles in an old notebook Polly's found in her bag. 'I get these . . .' Ma doesn't want to say visions. 'Spells. Dots, little black dots. Like flies.' Ma swallows, can't stop her tears. 'Do you ever get anything like that?'

'Flies? No. I see red a lot though – never was the easiest company.' Surprising herself again, Polly pats Ma's hand. 'I'm sure it won't be long, till your eyes are better.'

But what if they don't get better?

Little girls can get taken away, no matter how much they are loved, Ma's living proof. And Ma can't let dark thoughts and black visions take her Skye. Feeling Ma's loving eyes on her, Skye looks up, beaming as Ma shudders with emotion.

'Mum always did her best to get me back, but when I had those gaps in care, when she was really struggling, we desensitized. Too much time apart, till I never really knew her. Because there's no one,' Ma chokes out. 'I've no one. But her.'

Ma's right. Polly Jessen does see everything. Only in parallels, not judgements. Through her decades of self-inflicted distance, scores of neighbours, potential friendships, even daughters, came and went. While Polly was like Ma. Still like Ma. Scared and stubborn. Alone. Drowning in strangers.

Polly knows, too, the weight of being someone's world,

when you're the sole source of their sunshine. She's often thought of speaking to Ma, long before today, to try, but there's a forcefield around her, that Polly sees in herself, too. Ma's made herself an island; her only sustenance, that little girl.

But what pressure that can be, for the little ones as well.

'Just wait for those results,' Polly says. 'Till then, I've a good enough pair of eyes for the both of us.'

Community Conversations has worked. Indirectly.

Ma leaves the consulting room like she's come from a week-end pamper break, holding a sheet of white A4 to her chest. 'Floaters.' Ma stifles a giggle. 'What a word.' She hands out the paper, a referral request, direct to Moorfields. 'Those spells, the dots – I've been straining to see for weeks now, worried I'm losing my mind.' Ma sighs, relieved, relieved there's a solid reason for it all. She has the paper to prove it.

'Floaters?'

'Manifestations, in my rubbish vision.'

'Well, I'll be . . .'

Skye escapes from Polly's lap, reaching for Ma, leaving Polly dabbing her all too temporary good-enough pair of eyes with the cuff of her blouse.

'And best I'm off, now you're all right.' Adjusting her flip-flops, Polly stands, sniffs, careful not to give her whole self away. 'Who needs Community Conversations, when there's farts and floaters, anyway?'

But Ma won't let her wiggle out of it. 'And friendship.'

Eva Verde is a writer from Forest Gate, east London. She is of dual heritage. Identity and class are recurring themes throughout her work as she studies towards an MA in Prose Fiction. Her love song to libraries, 'I Am Not Your Tituba', forms part of Kit de Waal's *Common People: An Anthology of Working-Class Writers* with Unbound.

Eva's debut novel, *Lives Like Mine*, is published by Simon & Schuster in June 2021.

Eva lives in Essex with her husband, three daughters and Labrador sons.

Job Opportunity

by Richard Madeley

B ob Crawford stared at the single envelope on his door-
mat. It had the unmistakable markings of US Mail, and
his heart sank. He'd begun to associate these letters from
America with recurring episodes of disappointment and
failure. Why would this one be any different?

Bob tried to pull that morning's *Daily Express* from the
letterbox where the paper boy had crammed it. The half that
stuck out into the pouring rain on the other side of the door
was soaking wet. He managed to coax it through, but the
drenched section threatened to detach completely. He care-
fully carried the letter and the *Express* into his tiny, cramped
kitchen, and switched the kettle on.

Bob wasn't sure which to open first – newspaper or
envelope. It was, literally, 'his' newspaper. Bob had been an
Express reporter for two years now; he'd joined the daily on
his twenty-fifth birthday. Would the article he'd slaved over
and dropped into the chief sub-editor's wire basket twelve
hours ago have made the main edition? Would he even be
able to read it if it had? Half the newspaper collapsed in a

soggy heap on the kitchen floor. Maybe better to let it dry out for a bit, and examine the letter first. Using the butter knife next to the crumb-covered electric toaster, he roughly slit the envelope open. A single typewritten sheet fell out.

From the office of the Editor, Los Angeles Times
11/18/63

Dear Bob

Well, you're a persistent S.O.B. – I'll give you that. I haven't filed any of your previous letters but my headcount tells me your latest takes us into double figures.

So OK! Fine! You win! Come on over to L.A. and I'll see you. If I like you, I'll hire you, then and there. If I don't, I won't. Your risk with the airfare. Either way I'll wind up saving the paper some dough on airmail stamps.

We'll start with a test of your initiative. Your appointment in my office is Friday this week, 11.30am. I guess by the time you get this that'll give you a couple of days to get moving. Let's see how fast you can adapt to sudden opportunities in the land of opportunity, Bob. You keep telling me how much you've always wanted to work here. Your chance to prove it.

See you Friday. Don't be late. I mean it.

John Edwardes
Editor.

The hand that held the letter trembled slightly. This was it. This was IT. The opening he'd been hammering away at for months now. A chink in the blank wall of endless refusals.

Bob grabbed the coin jar on the kitchen top and shook out some pennies. He pulled the cord of his dressing gown tighter and went out into the shared hall of his apartment, where there was a public payphone. No time even to get dressed. Every second counted. This was Thursday morning. Allowing for the time difference, he had less than forty-eight hours to get to LA.

His first call was to the *Express* newsdesk. Lying fluently, and adopting a wheezy, throaty rasp, he called in sick. Early case of winter flu. Hoped to be back in a week or so. (That was a lie, too. If things went the way he intended in LA, Bob had no plans to return to Fleet Street.)

Next, he called BOAC's booking desk at London Airport. He scooped one of the last seats on a Boeing 707 leaving for California that afternoon.

Two minutes later he was in his bedsit, frantically packing and even more frantically searching for his passport. He eventually found it under a pile of blank expense forms.

Half an hour later, suited, booted, shaved and a single piece of hand-luggage packed, Bob took stock. Dollars? Check (cash left over from a working trip to Washington earlier that year). Business visa still in date? Check. Cheque book? Check. Clean shirt? Check. Spare tie? Check. Shaving kit and toothbrush? Check. Passport? He patted an inside jacket pocket. Check.

Time to go. It was still pouring outside, but Bob didn't care. Hailing a passing black cab and sinking damply into the back seat, he stared out at people scurrying along the pavements, umbrellas hoisted, raincoats buttoned to the chin, hopping and skipping over and around huge puddles. Let it rain. He was headed for the sunshine.

He was late. The 707 had been diverted mid-Atlantic to New York with fuel-feed problems that had slowed down the flight. For a few stomach-churning minutes Bob thought the passengers were going to be disembarked and made to board a different plane to continue their journey. His urgent questioning of a flight stewardess elicited the shattering news that this would probably result in being stuck in New York for anything up to ten hours. He'd never make the editor's deadline for arrival and something told him that this was a man with absolutely no time for excuses.

Just as despair was threatening to overwhelm him, the pilot announced over the PA that the fuel problem was fixed and they'd been given a departure slot in just over an hour. Estimated landing time in Los Angeles was 9.30am, Pacific Time. Bob did some fast sums. He wouldn't have to wait for any luggage, so once he'd cleared passport and immigration he could race to the airport's cab rank. Say, an hour from touchdown to taxi. The morning rush hour should be over by then. He doubted if the newspaper's offices in downtown LA could be more than an hour's drive away, tops. It was

going to be tight. It was going to be *very* tight. But he reck-
oned with luck and a following wind – literally, a tail wind,
if he was fortunate – he'd make it.

Flight time from New York to the west coast was six hours.
The 707 took off on schedule and for the first time since
they'd learned there was a problem back over the Atlantic,
Bob began to relax. He even slept for a while. He was woken
by the cabin announcement telling passengers to prepare
for landing. He looked at his watch, already wound back
for Pacific Time. Damn. Almost fifteen minutes later than
promised. No lucky tail wind, then.

Bob was the first to stand when the seatbelt lights went
out, and barged his way to the front of the plane. 'I'm sorry,
I'm sorry . . . I'm terribly late . . . I'm sorry . . . I have the most
urgent appointment . . . excuse me . . . I'm so sorry.'

He almost danced down the jetliner's steps and into the
covered walkway that led to the terminal building. He managed to snatch a glance at his watch as he settled into a steady
jog. Nine-fifty. An hour and forty minutes to get there. He
had to do it. He *had* to.

Passport and immigration control seemed an interminable
distance from the landing apron but Bob's luck took a turn for
the better when he arrived there. Booths were well staffed and
queues were short. He got through in about fifteen minutes
and broke into a jog again in the arrivals hall. He followed the
signs for taxis and exactly five minutes after having his passport stamped, he was climbing into the back of a Checker cab.

'Where to, bud?'

'*Los Angeles Times*, please. As fast as you can.'

'I ain't losin' my licence for no one, bud. Safe and steady gets us there, OK?'

Bob took a deep breath. 'Of course. I'm sorry. It's just that I'm terribly late for one of the most important appointments of my life. How long d'you think it'll take us to get there?'

The cab driver pulled away from the rank and glanced at the clock on his dashboard. 'Ten-twenty now. Reckon we'll be rolling up in an hour. That get you to the church on time, bud?'

'Yes. Thank you.'

'OK. So sit back, relax and enjoy the scenery. Next stop, *LA Times*.' The cab swerved into a filter lane and a few seconds later was cruising at a steady sixty down the freeway.

Bob sat back. But he didn't relax. He didn't enjoy the scenery, either. All he had eyes for was his wristwatch.

He had the fare ready in his hand as the cab pulled up outside the skyscraper domain of the *Los Angeles Times*.

'This is it, bud. Eleven twenty-five. That still good for ya?'

'Just about. Here.' He handed over a fistful of dollars. 'Keep the change. Goodbye.'

Bob heaved himself out of the back seat and ran across the pavement, waited impatiently for the revolving doors at the building's entrance to spin around enough to let him in, and strode across a marbled floor to the main reception desk.

There was one person ahead of him; a smartly dressed

man who seemed to be having an intense exchange with the receptionist. Bob looked impatiently around him. Despite his preoccupation, he sensed an atmosphere. Knots of people were talking in small, huddled groups. The sound of sobbing drifted across from somewhere. Before he could focus on any of it, the man in front of him moved away and Bob stepped up to the desk.

Immediately he noticed the blonde, bee-hived reception-ist had been crying. Twin tracks of mascara ran down her cheeks. Bob had no time to ask her why.

'My name's Bob Crawford. I'm from London. I have an appointment in' – he looked at his watch for the hundredth time that morning – 'in two minutes, with the editor. I can't be late.'

She nodded, dabbing her eyes and consulting a large appointments diary in front of her.

'Yes, sir, Mr Crawford. Take the elevator over there' – she gestured with a shaking hand that held the tissue – 'and go to level seventeen. I'll ring ahead and say you're on the way up.'

For the first time since he'd exited the plane, Bob walked, not ran. He strolled calmly to the lifts. He was on time. He'd made it, although without a second to spare. Thank God. Thank *God*.

Seventeen floors up he stepped out of the lift and into a luxurious outer office. This one had a reception desk too, with another bee-hived blonde, almost identical to the one downstairs, sitting behind it.

Bob approached, smiling. 'Hello! I'm Bob Crawford. I'm

here to see the ed—' He stopped, shocked. *This* woman was crying, too. More mascara on her cheeks, more damp, screwed-up tissues on the table in front of her.

'I'm sorry ... what's going on?' he asked, his smile of triumph and relief fading. 'Everyone seems very ... well ... *upset* here this morning. What's happened? What's wrong?'

She stared at him from red-rimmed eyes.

'Haven't you heard, Mr Crawford? Haven't you *heard*?'

'No. Heard what? What haven't I heard? Tell me.'

She looked as if she was going to start crying again, but managed to gather herself before replying.

'It's our president. He's been shot. Shot dead. Just an hour past.'

Bob's mind raced. *Shit*. He'd done a fair amount of research on the *LA Times*'s editorial team, but he hadn't really bothered with its corporate structure. Who the fuck was president of the company that owned the newspaper? He hadn't the faintest idea and he was about to meet the bloody editor. He opened his mouth to ask the receptionist for the man's name but at that moment the door to the editor's inner sanctum burst open and the man himself stood there staring at him.

'You Bob?'

'Yes.'

'John Edwardes. I'd say pleased to meet with you, but can't say I'll ever be pleased about anything again. You heard what's just happened?'

Bob nodded. 'Yes ... your president's been shot. I'm so sorry. Such sad news.'

The editor stared at him. His glasses were pushed back on his forehead, shirtsleeves rolled back above the elbows, tie undone and hair awry.

'Sad news? Jeez, you Brits really are the masters of understatement.' He shook his head. 'I'm sorry, Bob, this meet is gonna have to wait. Come back next week, say Tuesday. It's gonna be fucking pandemonium around here for a while.'

Bob was unable to hide his disappointment. 'But I've come all the way from London. I've been travelling nonstop since I got your letter . . . I moved heaven and earth to get here on time, Mr Edwardes. I . . .' He stopped, defeated.

The editor held up both hands. 'OK, OK, I guess I can give you five minutes, but we'll have to hold the main meet. Come through.'

Bob followed him into a plush office and was waved to the squashy leather chair opposite the editor's desk. Edwardes sank into his own seat and rubbed the heels of both hands into his eyes.

'Jeez, I still cannot believe this has happened. You heard the details?'

Bob shook his head. 'No, just that your president's been shot.'

'Yeah, well, of course you wouldn't know much yet. I only got an insider briefing just now because my chief reporter has a great contact in the Feds.' The editor paused, shaking his head in disbelief. 'Sniper, they think.'

A *sniper*? Bob had assumed this was a case of a robbery gone wrong, or maybe a domestic incident. But a sharpshooter?

For a corporate chief? He made a decision. Maybe it wasn't such a terrible lapse of research not to know who the top man was. He'd come clean.

'Look . . . I'm terribly sorry not to know this . . . but what was your president's name?'

The next few minutes, Bob would say later, were a kind of blur. Being frogmarched from the editor's office by the man himself. Shoved into the lift with a parting: 'Call yourself a frigging *reporter*? You don't even know our president's goddamned *name*!' A burly security guard meeting him as he emerged at the ground floor, bodily ejecting him from the building on to the pavement.

There, he saw a newspaper vendor standing at traffic lights, hawking the first editions of specially rushed-out editions of the *LA Times* to drivers as they stopped on red.

The massive, screaming front-page headline.

JFK ASSASSINATED IN DALLAS!

Bob stared at it for a long, long time. Eventually he turned away and flagged down a cab.

'Where to, bud?'

'Airport, please. There's no rush.'

Author's note. This is a true story. Only the names have been changed. Except the one at the end.

Richard Madeley left school at sixteen to be a cub reporter on his local paper. By nineteen he was a deputy editor, and that same year joined BBC local radio in the newsroom. He went on to work as a reporter/presenter for Border Television, Yorkshire Television (where he covered the Peter Sutcliffe serial murders) and Granada Television, meeting fellow reporter and wife-to-be Judy Finnigan. The two went on to launch ITV's *This Morning* programme, and after thirteen years joined Channel Four for their eponymous teatime series, which ran for eight years. Richard now works as a freelance, covering for Piers Morgan on *Good Morning Britain*, Michael Ball on Radio 2, and live talkRADIO programmes. He has written three *Sunday Times* top-ten bestsellers and is currently working on his fourth novel. He and his wife have run the hugely influential Richard & Judy Book Club in association with WHSmith since 2010. They have also written their double-page column for Saturday's *Daily Express* since 2000 and Richard is the *Daily Telegraph*'s Agony Uncle, with a full-page weekly column.

The Wrong Cake

by Katie Fforde

'I do understand the concept of "stuck in traffic",' said Betsy into her phone. 'How far away are you? Gah!' He must have gone into a tunnel, she thought as she was cut off.

'That didn't sound good,' said the only other person in the foyer, an attractive man in a suit, who she took to be the manager of the hotel.

Had she groaned out loud? She hadn't meant to. 'It's the worst! The cake that I've made for a wedding today probably won't get here in time.' She threw her hands in the air in despair. 'Then the bride will go on to my website to leave a dreadful review, and my tiny, precious business will die!'

The manager seemed confused. 'I'm sorry. When I saw you, I thought you were one of the bridesmaids.'

She gave a rueful laugh. 'It's the orange dress that suits no one – a dead giveaway! But I also made the cake. And I care more about that because that's my business. I'm only a bridesmaid for today. Thank goodness.'

Thinking of the bridezilla upstairs in a bridal suite, sur-rounded by a make-up artist, a hair-dresser and a troupe of her 'closest friends' made Betsy shudder. Did Chelsea have some sort of hold over them all, like she did over Betsy, because she was making the cake and needed a good review? At least the dresses had pockets they could slip a phone into. But it turned out this was so the bride's attendants could be summoned at any time, even from the ladies' loo.

She'd been surprised to be asked to be a bridesmaid – she had only met Chelsea recently through a mutual friend. But when she'd been told that all the bridesmaids had to chip in for the bride's spa day she understood why so many had been asked. The spa had been outrageously expensive. Betsy had been heartily relieved that she had a genuine reason not to go, so only had to contribute to Chelsea's five-star package that cost the same as a small second-hand car, without having to shell out for her own as well.

If only she'd just agreed to do the cake and not got sucked into being a bridesmaid, she could have just delivered the cake and not involved anyone else. But she'd been delayed finishing it and the icing needed to set before she could transport it so she'd had to ask her brother to help. What could she do to save this situation now?

'There's a lovely cake for the wedding that's happening a couple of hours from now, in the orangery at the other end of the house,' said the manager, 'but I don't suppose that helps.'

Betsy's mind whirled like a fidget spinner. 'I think that could help a lot!'

'I really don't see how,' he replied. 'I'm Rob, by the way.'

'Betsy. Couldn't we quickly borrow it? Just for the photos! Unless it's totally different, of course. Chelsea probably won't remember what she ordered, she wasn't all that interested.' This was a genius idea. 'We'll just let them get the shots and then whisk the cake away. It'll be fine! As long as there's a picture of the bride and groom with the cake, that's all that matters!' She stared at Rob, hoping that as the manager of the hotel he would do this for her.

'But won't they want a picture of them cutting the cake?' he objected.

'They can't have it! I'll stop them!'

'How? By throwing yourself between the knife and the cake?' Rob didn't look impressed.

'Whatever it takes! My business depends on this.'

'Won't your bride be angry?'

Betsy shrugged dramatically. 'She probably won't notice. I mean, she'll have had a glass or two of prosecco by then. It'll be fine!' She wasn't nearly as sure as she sounded but she needed him on side if there was a chance her plan would work. 'So, could you show me this other cake?'

He led her through the big former stately home, now one of the most fashionable wedding venues in the area, until they came to the orangery.

The cake had been placed at the end, with views on to the garden, full of flowers although not, at this moment, sunshine.

Betsy peered closely at the cake. It was fairly conventional: three tiers, decorated with flowers, and more flowers on top instead of a model bride and groom. 'It's not bad. Mine's better, of course, but luckily Chelsea didn't want a bride and groom on top either, so she probably won't notice it isn't hers.' Her phone vibrated in her pocket. She hoped it would be her brother saying he'd arrived, but it was Chelsea, demanding to know where she was.

'I'm going to have to go. Chelsea's noticed I'm not there, which is "not acceptable". Be a love and help me put the cake in the ballroom, where Chelsea wants it, and then I must dash upstairs. Please?'

Betsy fixed Rob with her most serious gaze. 'Chelsea will take me down online if there's no cake. Anything that stops that is a good plan. Even if it does seem a bit dodgy to you.' She gave him a grateful smile. 'If you can sort me out with this, I'll make a cake for you, whatever kind you like.'

He looked taken aback. 'That would be nice but—'

'I'm just so grateful to you for helping.' She smiled again. 'And you'll be on hand to get the cake back afterwards?'

'I'll do everything I can.'

A couple of thoughts occurred to Betsy as she made her way to the lift. One was how unfair it was that you only ever met nice men when you weren't in a position to do anything about it, and the other was why was he doubtful about being able to help? As hotel manager, or even assistant manager, shouldn't that have been easy?

Considering Chelsea was getting ready in the same building as the ceremony was taking place, it was amazing how late she managed to be. Umpteen problems so small only the bride could see them had to be dealt with before, finally, Chelsea was ready to meet her groom and actually get married.

Betsy decided that if she was ever running a hotel, she'd have a bridal cut-off time. More than half an hour late and the wedding would be cancelled. She'd suggest it to Rob when she gave him his 'thank you' cake.

Betsy made a note which bridesmaid she was supposed to walk behind as they all crammed into the second lift. The wedding dress was so enormous only Chelsea and her two closest friends could fit in the first one.

The wedding planner was awaiting their arrival and she arranged everyone into position. Betsy was happy to be the last in the line-up as it meant she could peel off and deal with the cake. Thank goodness the wedding planner hadn't noticed it hadn't been there earlier.

'Just make sure you walk directly behind me and don't smile at your friends in the audience!' ordered Chelsea, and they were off.

After an embarrassingly long and sentimental exchange of vows and the other formalities came the photographs. Mostly they involved only the bride and groom but Chelsea, with her unique appetite for making everyone else do what she wanted, required her team of women dressed in orange to be there too.

Betsy was delighted. It meant she'd be there when the photographs with the cake were taken and afterwards she could whisk it away, run through the house and get the cake back to its place in the orangery.

Then the sun came out after all, and the photographer got everyone to go outside. The bridesmaids had to stand in tiers on the stone steps leading to the house; they had to stand at Chelsea's feet and gaze up at her adoringly while she stood on a plinth; they had to lean out longingly towards the rowing boat in which Chelsea and her groom floated towards an island.

'If she'd been paying us,' said Julie, another bridesmaid who Betsy had got to know fairly well during all the hanging about beforehand, 'she'd have got value for money.'

'Mm,' agreed Betsy. 'It's amazing that she managed to bully a group of strong-minded women into doing what she wanted and paying for the privilege. We had to pay for our dresses, the hen do, the wedding present, travel to and from, and probably the overnight stay.' Betsy was avoiding this by going home at the first opportunity.

'You were lucky,' said Julie. 'We had to pay for the minibus to pick us up from the station. I reckon this wedding has cost me at least five hundred pounds and we're not even close friends!'

When the wedding planner announced that the guests couldn't be kept waiting any longer, everyone went back inside.

Inevitably Betsy's hyper-alertness about what was happening to the cake was softened by a meal and a couple of glasses of prosecco. But something made her look up, only to notice the bride and groom leaving the table although they hadn't had the speeches yet. Then Betsy saw the photographer and the wedding planner; they were going to photograph the cake! Those sitting on either side of her must have thought there was a medical emergency as she leaped from her seat. She arrived by the cake panting. Although she needn't have rushed. Apparently they needed about thirty shots of the couple holding the knife, clinging on to each other, about to plunge the knife into the smooth icing.

'Right, nearly there,' said the photographer. 'We'll just take one or two of you cutting the cake and then you can get back for the speeches.'

'No!' said Betsy. 'You can't cut it.'

'What do you mean, I can't cut it?' demanded Chelsea.

'It's not your cake.'

She hadn't meant to come out with it. She'd meant to find some other excuse.

The explosion was terrifying. 'It's not my cake?' Chelsea exploded, and then continued with a torrent of abuse that embarrassed everyone. Betsy stood there with her head bowed, hoping she wasn't going to cry. Her business would be ruined now.

Just then, Rob appeared, panting slightly with a slight smudge of icing on his jacket. 'It's all right! This is your cake. Go ahead and cut it.'

Betsy stood there gaping until Rob took her shoulder and led her gently away. 'Your brother turned up with the cake while you were at the ceremony. I switched them but couldn't find you to tell you.'

She felt so relieved that she collapsed against him. He

supported her while she took some deep breaths. Then the groom appeared.

'Is there a problem?' he asked.

'Betsy thought there was,' said Rob, 'but she didn't realize it had been resolved. I think you'll find that the cake's delicious and you'll be a hundred per cent satisfied with it.'

Rob led her from the room into the foyer.

'How can I ever thank you enough?' said Betsy, overcome with gratitude.

'You can return the favour. I'm the best man for the other wedding and I haven't got a plus one. Care to come with me?'

'So you're not—'

'Not the hotel manager, no.'

'And yet you did all that for me? Switching the cakes? Making everything all right?'

'I couldn't bear to think of your business being damaged because of someone being held up in traffic.' His eyes crinkled as he smiled.

She smiled back, suddenly a bit breathless. He was gorgeous!

'Now, are you up for another wedding – in about an hour? I can't guarantee how good the cake will be.'

'I'd love to come. Shall I wear jeans? Or an orange dress?'

Katie Fforde lives in Gloucestershire and is the author of about thirty novels including *A Springtime Affair* and *A Rose Petal Summer*. When not writing she enjoys her garden, her family and her grandchildren.

Blind Dates

by Dorothy Koomson

It's the potential for adventure I've missed the most.

That's why I'm doing this. Dating. Blind dating. There's no way on Earth I'd normally do this, but after a less than ideal eighteen months or so – starting well before world events conspired to transform everyone's lives – I'd had a long, hard, completely unflattering look at my life and I found it merely satisfactory.

It worked, yes. I had lots of positive ticks in my life:

Flat. ✔

Job. ✔

Friends. ✔

Hobbies. ✔

But nothing amazing or special. Where was the adventure? Where was the excitement of the unknown because I was hurtling headlong into something that was so completely different to what I knew? Nowhere, that's where.

Hence getting dressed up, wearing my best make-up, creating my most elaborate hairdo, and walking into a hotel restaurant to meet a man I don't know for dinner.

I'm forty-five and I haven't been in a long-term relationship since Jerry and I ended our college romance that lasted three years after we graduated. In that time he's been married and divorced – twice – and I've not even come close to settling with anyone.

The bar where I perch on the high, padded stool is glossy and stylish. Lots of mirrors and shininess, sharp corners, plush materials on the seats. I'm trying to look relaxed, as if I often get all dressed up and take myself off to a bar on a Tuesday evening.

Most of the time, I don't care what people think of me, I don't care if they stare, but today I don't want them to think – correctly – that I'm on a date then *pity* me. Those 'oh, isn't she brave trying to find love *at her age*' sympathy glances are intolerable.

There is nothing to pity me for. I'm literally here because I want to meet someone who wants to do stuff like walk the coast road, try to create a new beer, or run a 10K (my body is going nowhere near a marathon).

Actually, I'm here because my friends picked a man for me from a dating app and I'm curious enough to go along with it.

I'm not even that bothered about the 'physical' side of things. Getting *that* is easy, especially if you're not bothered about anything beyond getting to the final, ecstatic destination. And love?

What is love? A unique, euphoric feeling that you experience when you meet 'The One' and that you hope lasts and lasts until all the days have reached your forever? To be honest, that sounds too nebulous, too uncertain for me to hitch any part of my life to. I'm not against love, but I won't feel like I'm missing out if I don't find it.

'What can I get you?' the bartender asks.

'Cranberry and soda,' a female voice says beside me.

My head snaps round to look at her, a little outraged that she's jumped the queue for drinks when I was in here first.

She's got that extra bit of make-up on, her dress is sleek, sophisticated as well as pretty and flattering, while her hair has been styled to flatter the lines of her face.

'Oh, sorry,' she says with a smile, 'are you waiting? I didn't see you. I'm so nervous . . . I'm here for a blind date. Haven't been on one in years. Years. Don't know why I decided now would be a good time. Oh, and not sure why I decided to tell you – a complete stranger – all about my quest for love.'

She grins again, then waves her hand in a way that says I should step forward and order my drink, now that she knows I was here first.

The barman is unimpressed that she has paused to speak to me while ordering a drink.

'Snap,' I say to the woman beside me.

'Snap?' she replies.

I'm suddenly acutely aware of the barman and how I do

not want to be pitied by him for being on a blind date. 'I mean, your drink. Snap.'

'Cranberry and soda, right?' the bartender says.

'Erm ... right ... except maybe swap the cranberry for vodka and the soda for orange? And while you're at it, grab a cranberry and soda for my friend here.'

The barman barely conceals his irritation before he moves away.

I lower my voice and speak to the woman beside me. 'I meant snap because I'm on a blind date, too.'

'Oh!' she exclaims, then lowers her voice. 'Oh, fantastic! It's not just me then who never got around to *grand amour* and adventure.'

'I guess not.'

The bartender returns with our drinks and, quick as a flash, she has her card out and is paying.

'Thank you,' I say, 'I'll get the next one.'

'You are most welcome.'

'How long have you been speaking to the person you're meeting?' I ask.

'I know nothing about him – my friends set the whole thing up through a dating app. I've got a general description and name and that's about it.'

'Me too.'

'Oh my goodness, this is too spooky! Imagine if we're here on a date with the same man?'

This thought widens my eyes. 'What's his name?'

'Ted?' she says.

No, surely not. 'Mine is called Edward—'

'Which is basically the same name.' She covers her burgundy-coloured lips with her hand. 'Oh, this is *so* the sort of thing that happens to me. All right, what description does he have?'

'Medium-height and light-haired?' I reply.

'Oh, phew! Mine is tall and dark.'

'Right. He sounds more my type, to be honest,' I admit.

'Yours sounds like my type, too.'

'What's your name, woman who could be me?'

'Gayle,' she says.

'I'm Michaela,' I reply.

'What do we do if they walk in and we prefer each other's man?' Gayle asks.

'Pretend to be the other one,' I joke.

'No, we couldn't do that. *Could we?*'

'No!' I look around us in case anyone is sitting close enough to hear. 'We couldn't do that. I was joking.'

'Oh, right. Joking. Yeah.'

I'm about to say something else when the door opens and two men step through. Medium-height, light-haired for me. Tall and dark for her.

And the one for her is *beautiful.* Exactly how my dream man would look – smooth dark skin, no hair and the most amazing mouth that I can't stop myself wondering what it would be like to kiss. *Snap out of it!* I tell myself. *You're here to meet Edward.* It's not his fault that I'm uninterested in him, while Gayle looks as though she would leap into his arms given half a chance.

'Are you absolutely sure we can't pretend to be each other?' Gayle asks under her breath.

'Yes,' I say miserably, 'I'm absolutely sure.'

'You might have seen me on television?' Edward says with a small proud smile, while I pick at my dinner. The food is delicious, and Edward is ... I don't know what Edward is like really, because I keep looking over at the other table.

I try to tell myself not to, that it's none of my damn business, and that Edward deserves better, but I can't help it.

'Hmm-hmm,' I reply to Edward, nodding my head.

'Oh, you've seen it? Oh, fantastic.' The surprise and happiness in his voice forces the brakes on my rudeness and makes me focus on him.

'Which version of the ad was your favourite? The long version or the short version?'

'Erm ...' I reply, frantically racking my brains to see if I remember seeing his face on telly. No, nothing.

Edward's brow furrows as he stares at me. He has nice eyes; they are kind, lived in, loved in. And he is good-looking – if I'd met him in any other circumstance we might have had a chance.

'I'm sorry,' I say, shamefaced. 'I haven't seen you on television.'

He turns his head towards the other table, which I can see over his shoulder. 'You'd rather be over there, wouldn't you?'

'It's not what you think,' I say, the words sounding pathetic as they come out of my mouth: I'm on a date with a nice man and I'm concentrating on someone who probably doesn't know I exist.

'Don't worry, I saw how you looked at that guy when he walked in. I was kind of the same about your friend,' he admits, looking sheepish.

'Oh, she's not my friend,' I say quickly. I would never even consider what I'm considering if she were. There are lines you don't cross, things you wouldn't dream of when you're someone's friend.

At that moment, Gayle looks behind her and we catch each other's eye. I feel the heat of embarrassment rush through my body; she obviously picked up on me constantly eye-balling them from across the room. She turns back to her date, who, I must admit miserably, she seems to be getting on very well with.

'They're getting on really well. I think she really likes him. Well, he is *really* handsome.'

'Oh, great, thanks,' Edward says.

'As are you,' I say with a wince.

He shakes his head and smiles. 'Shall we just call it a night?' he says.

'Yes, that'd probably be for the best,' I say eagerly, and I put my hand up to call the waiter.

'Wow, you really know how to make a guy feel good about himself,' he laughs. And it is a rich, warm sound that makes me smile.

'Don't give me that, I haven't forgotten you've basically

said you prefer that woman over there to me, so let's quit while we're behind.'

'Fair point,' he concedes. He seems like such a nice guy, it's a real shame there's no spark between us.

We wave at Gayle and Ted on the way out, and Gayle momentarily sticks out her bottom lip as if to say she's slightly envious that I'm leaving with 'her' guy.

Outside, the air is fragrantly warm and the night is velvety black. Edward and I share an awkward half-hug, exchange numbers because you never know, before he wanders off down the road in the direction I would normally go in, which means I have to pretend I'm going in the opposite direction.

As I walk down the dark streets of Brighton, the sea is constantly gushing in the distance, reminding me that it is there and it is going to be there forever.

When enough time has passed for Edward to have got a taxi home, I head back the way I came. I don't have to, I can walk back to the bus stop another way, but I have to pass the restaurant and see if their date lasted longer than mine; if they're going to take it any further.

I've also come back this way because I've come to a big decision: if they're there, then I'm going to make a move.

Ted is climbing into a taxi when I turn the corner, leaving Gayle alone on the pavement. She grins at him as the taxi pulls away and waves until it is out of sight.

'Bit tight of him to leave you alone to get a taxi,' I say to Gayle.

'Oh no, I insisted. He lives over in Crawley, it'll take him ages to get back.' She looks quizzically at me. 'So how was your date?'

'Not as good as it could have been,' I admit.

'Because of Ted? He told me he fancied you. He actually gave me his number to pass on to you in case it didn't work out with Edward.'

'Same with Edward – gave me his number to pass on to you.'

'Oh, hilarious! We totally should have just swapped. Ted kept asking me if I would mind if he dated my friend. He wouldn't believe me when I said we'd only met tonight.'

'Well, about that ... That's why I came back. Ted wasn't the main reason why I didn't get on with Edward ... it was you. You've heard people talking about bromances, right?'

She nods.

'It's like that with you, but a sister version. A sisomance? Is that a thing? Could it be a thing? I don't know. All I know is I kept looking over at you two thinking, *I want to be sitting where Ted is so I can find out everything about Gayle and I bet she doesn't even know I exist.*'

'Really? 'Cos I was totally thinking the same thing! I kept wishing we could ditch the guys and go get a drink somewhere because we'd have such a laugh.'

I almost explode with happiness. 'Let's go for a drink.'

'Yes!' Gayle exclaims. 'I have so much I want to ask you.'

'Like, what's our first adventure going to be?'

'Absolutely. Skydiving sounds good to me!'

'I like a person who thinks big on the first go,' I laugh.

'But of course! This is going to be best. The absolute best.'

I can't help smiling, because I know she's absolutely right.

Dorothy Koomson is the multi-award-winning author of seventeen bestselling novels and has been making up stories since she was thirteen. Her books include: *All My Lies Are True*, *The Ice Cream Girls*, *Tell Me Your Secret*, *The Brighton Mermaid*, *My Best Friend's Girl* and *The Chocolate Run*. Both *The Ice Cream Girls* and her Quick Reads book *The Beach Wedding* were World Book Night titles. After living in Australia, Dorothy now lives in Brighton.

Blind Justice

by Vaseem Khan

'A blind man? How can a blind man rob a bank?'

'He didn't *rob* the bank. Not in the sense that you mean.' Irritation flashed across Joshi's glistening brow. 'And we're not a bank. Not exactly.'

Not exactly. Chopra looked thoughtfully at the man opposite him. Joshi was a bear, dressed in a navy safari suit, saddlebags of sweat under the arms. The air-conditioner was out again and the office was sweltering. May in Mumbai, just before the monsoon. The rains were late and the city broiled in the heat.

'We're a lending agency,' clarified Joshi. 'We lend money.'

'Who do you lend it to?'

'Whoever needs it the most.' There was something evasive in the man's manner, Chopra thought. Thirty years on the police force had left him with a sense for such things. The only difference between *that* job and *this*: you could choose your clients in a private detective agency. Nevertheless ...

'What exactly did Imran Mirza take?'

'Documents. Valuable documents.'

Chopra watched him swat away a fly. 'And why do you suspect him?'

'Because I terminated his position at the agency a month ago. He was . . . unhappy.'

'Revenge?'

'Revenge,' nodded Joshi, emphatically.

The lending agency was housed on the ground floor of a rundown, whitewashed concrete bunker on the very out-skirts of the city. Paint flaked from the exterior walls, and a lopsided banner hung over the front door. Dogs dozed in the shadows.

It had taken an hour to drive through Mumbai's mid-morning traffic, a chaos of blaring horns, buzzing rickshaws, suicidal motorcyclists and the occasional bullock cart. Urban India in the twenty-first century, a gridlocked vision of Dante's hell.

Chopra parked the jeep and turned off the engine, and with it, the rattling air-conditioner. He cracked a window for his young ward, shuffling around impatiently in the back.

Almost ten months after the one-year-old elephant had arrived on his doorstep, Chopra continued to marvel at the surreal nature of the situation. Here he was, a retired policeman in his late forties, driving around the city with an elephant calf in tow. Anywhere else in the world it would be ludicrous. But this was India. There were far stranger sights on the streets of a place like Mumbai. That was the thing about a city of twenty million souls – there were just as many tales to tell.

He got out and walked into the premises, his shirt sticking to his back.

Joshi had left it to a junior to show him around.

There was little to see.

A warren of tiny offices, kitted out with ancient furniture, wobbling ceiling fans, dented steel filing cabinets and a sense of hopelessness radiating from the bare walls. What had he expected? He'd already guessed that the agency was the way station of last resort for those in desperate need of funds. There were many such operations around the country catering to those that fell outside the regular banking system. In the old days, the same function would have been fulfilled by ruthless feudal moneylenders – in villages up and down the country, it still was.

'Where were the files stolen from?'

The flunky introduced himself as Peter Fernandes then led him through to a room populated exclusively by steel almirahs, at least a dozen of them. He pointed at one of the tall cabinets. 'He took the documents from that one.'

To Chopra, it looked identical to the rest. He moved closer and examined the almirah, focusing on the lock. He noticed something and brushed his fingers over the galvanized steel.

'The lock wasn't forced,' added Fernandes. 'We think he picked it.'

Chopra raised an eyebrow. 'So a blind man somehow broke into this place, found his way to this exact cabinet, *and* picked the lock?'

The man had the decency to look embarrassed.

'Who has the keys?'

'Only Mr Joshi. When we need a file, we take the keys from him, then return them immediately.'

Chopra paused, his thoughts ticking over in the silence. 'How long did Mirza work here?'

'Fifteen years, I think.'

'Why was he sacked?'

Fernandes's pencil moustache twitched. 'Perhaps you should ask Mr Josh—'

'I'm asking you.'

'Well, ah, I believe it was incompetence. He just wasn't very good at his job.'

'And yet they kept him around for fifteen years.'

Mirza lived a short, ten-minute drive from the agency's offices.

Chopra slurped on a Coke as he waited at a set of traffic lights. Any time now he expected the air-conditioner to surrender to the rising heat. A trunk snaked from the rear of the van and curled itself around the can.

'Are you thirsty, boy?' He watched in the mirror as the little elephant upended the can into his mouth.

The elephant had been sent to him by his long-vanished uncle. Beyond that he had managed to learn very little about his new charge. Neither had accommodating the beast into his life proved an easy task, but his wife, Poppy, had been insistent. In the end, he'd put him into a walled compound – complete with mango tree and mud wallow – at the rear of the restaurant he'd opened following his retirement from the force. The restaurant now doubled as the offices for his fledgling detective agency, which he had named after the animal: the Baby Ganesh Agency.

One thing he couldn't deny: Ganesha had proved a lucky charm on the various investigations he'd taken up since opening the agency.

'What do you think?' he mused. 'Could a blind man really have done it?'

Ganesha threw the empty can over his shoulder, then reached over with his trunk to poke at the radio dials.

The little elephant had a fondness for music.

Imran Mirza, in the flesh, was a small man with sunken cheeks and tufted grey hair like a hatchling. His bungalow was tiny, but clean, and neatly appointed.

They sat in the living room. The ceiling fan ruffled Chopra's moustache.

'They didn't sack me because I was incompetent,' said Mirza. 'They sacked me because I went blind.' His knuckles tightened on his white cane. 'I began to lose my sight a year ago. When it eventually became clear to Joshi that I would become almost completely blind, he decided to let me go. Made up a story about incompetence, even though I was still perfectly capable of doing my job.'

'What *was* your job?'

'I was a loan officer. People – mainly from the villages – would come into the agency needing money. I would explain what we could do for them, then lead them through the formalities. The more I could get them to borrow, the higher my bonus. I was very good at my job.'

Mirza's self-loathing was evident. Chopra didn't need intuition or a policeman's instincts to understand that this was a confession, of sorts.

'Why did Joshi really sack you?'

The edges of Mirza's mouth curled upwards. 'How would you like to go for a little drive?'

In the jeep, Mirza allowed Ganesha to run his trunk over his face.

In return, the elephant calf stood still as the blind man twisted around in his seat and ran his hands over his knobbly skull and gently flapping ears. 'You know, in foreign countries they use guide dogs to help people like me. I wonder if anyone's thought of using elephants?'

Chopra smiled. The elephant had proved to be a sound judge of character over the past ten months. If Imran Mirza had painted a favourable impression with his young ward then it was a good bet the man was not the villain Joshi had made him out to be.

His smile vanished as a man herding goats drifted nonchalantly into the middle of the road, instantly inciting chaos. He hammered the horn, cursing under his breath.

They arrived in the village twenty minutes later, a collection of whitewashed huts slapped together out of brick and mud and thatch, no different to a dozen such hamlets dotted around the city's periphery. Fields of wheat, turned brown by the blowtorch of the sun, hazed into the distance.

A bullock sat under the shade of a tamarind tree, slapping flies from its rump, looking on curiously as he parked the jeep.

Chopra and Ganesha followed Mirza as he tapped his way across a dusty quadrangle, curious eyes following the little party.

Mirza led them to a hut at the very outskirts of the village. Beyond, Chopra could see a barren field, collapsed levees and the relic of an ancient plough.

Inside the hut, a woman crouched beside a stove, sari hitched up to her knees, blowing at the embers of a fire under a steel pot. A young boy squatted beside her. On a rope charpoy, a small baby cried in staccato bursts.

The woman shot to her feet in alarm as Mirza and Chopra entered, Ganesha pausing at the door.

'Don't be frightened, Parvati,' said Mirza. 'This is a friend.'

Friend, thought Chopra. A strange way to characterize the man trying to assess your complicity in a crime.

The woman said nothing, waiting, seemingly for further instruction from Mirza. The blind man waved a hand at the inside of the tiny hut. 'Take a good look, Chopra. This is how hundreds of millions still live in this new India of ours.'

Chopra wondered what the man's point was.

The sap now flowing through India's veins had yet to make its way to every section of society, that was simply a fact of life. The unholy trinity of globalization, outsourcing and westernization may have transformed urban India, but the hinterlands still laboured under the legacy of millennia-old inequalities. That wasn't about to change overnight.

'This is Parvati,' continued Mirza. 'Her husband, Rajesh, was a farmer. A tiny plot, just enough to feed his family. He bought the plot using money that we lent him. That *I* lent him. A year ago, I foreclosed on his loan. He'd had a run of bad crops. Dry weather. Pestilence. The land out there now belongs to Joshi. But he has no wish to farm it. He's waiting for the price to go up so he can sell it. As Mumbai continues to grow, no doubt soon it will swallow this village and someone will try to build a mall here.'

He fell momentarily silent.

Chopra's eyes followed the boy – he could have been no more than five – as he emerged from behind his mother and skipped out of the hut to play with Ganesha. The elephant picked up a stick and began duelling with him. Squeals of laughter erupted from the child.

'After I took his land from him, Rajesh came to our offices. He poured kerosene on to his clothes and set himself alight. He died from his burns.'

Another silence, broken by the sounds of the boy's laughter and a soft bugling note from Ganesha.

'It wasn't your fault,' said Chopra, and realized that he meant it. He saw that the woman was silently weeping.

Mirza stirred, then tapped his way to the corner of the room. He bent and reached inside a steel trunk, then came back with a bundle of manila files wrapped in string. He dropped the files at Chopra's feet, raising a small puff of dust.

'Two hundred files in total,' said the blind man. 'Two hundred lives. If I could have carried more, I would have.'

'You planned it for a long time,' said Chopra. 'If I had to guess, I'd say you took the keys from Joshi well before you were sacked and made copies. Keys to the office *and* to the filing cabinet. You knew which cabinet to target on the night you snuck back in to take those files because you left marks around the lock. Little dents. A sort of Braille.'

Mirza flashed a humourless smile. 'Joshi sacked me because I asked him to act in good conscience. After Rajesh died I asked him to help Parvati and her children. Instead, he took her land.'

'And now what? Do you think that by stealing these files you can save her? Save all these people's farms?'

'Joshi doesn't trust computers. These files are the only record that any of them owe the agency a thing. If I destroy them, I will set two hundred families free.'

Chopra stared at him, and then, because he understood the urge that powered Imran Mirza's actions, a desire to balance the scales, to seek justice in a nation where justice so often eluded the poor and the powerless, because he understood what it meant to light a candle in the darkness, he smiled.

'You know,' he said, 'I don't think I'm going to take this case, after all.'

He turned and headed back outside where a young boy and a young elephant played beneath the late afternoon sun.

Vaseem Khan is the author of two crime series set in India, the *Baby Ganesh Agency* series, and the *Malabar House* historical crime novels. His first book, *The Unexpected Inheritance of Inspector Chopra*, was a *Times* bestseller, now translated into fifteen languages. In 2018, he was awarded the *Eastern Eye* Arts, Culture and Theatre Award for Literature. Vaseem was born in London, but spent a decade working in India.

A Slightly Open Marriage

by Helen Lederer

The cream cheese on the carrot cake was the first chance at sensual pleasure Mary had enjoyed for weeks. The more frosting that went into her mouth, the easier it was to manage her anger about Gary. Not only had her husband managed to spill his Chinese takeaway over a curtain she'd made for a client, but he'd lied about it as well.

Gary had slammed out of the house before she'd finished shouting, leaving her no choice but to follow him out on to the drive in her slippers. She might still be there now, screaming at the back of his motorbike, had Sandra not lured her next door with the offer of a gratis cake at her coffee morning.

Given her raised blood pressure, the very least she could do was get a bit of succour from the tasty cream-cheese icing. She found herself holding the cake stand in one hand in case anyone else had the same idea.

'It's very moreish, isn't it?'

A woman in a pinafore dress had walked round to Mary's side of the cake table. 'What is?' asked Mary.

'The frosting – that was on top of the cake?'

Even Mary had to admit the top of the carrot cake was now looking quite bald. But she didn't appreciate being made to feel guilty by a stranger. She wondered if she should let Sandra know that one of her friends had just made her feel that she'd shoplifted from a food bank. But Sandra was still outside in the garden, forcing paper napkins on her guests who didn't appear to want them.

'I'm Clara. I live two streets away.' Clara held out her hand.

Mary felt obliged to wipe a frosted finger on one of Sandra's napkins, before accepting it.

'I'm Mary. I live next door.'

Mary was surprised at the length of Clara's plait, which seemed a bold choice for someone over six foot tall. There might be a danger of whiplash if she turned round quickly.

Clara suddenly lowered her voice. 'I'm a therapist. Well, counsellor, really.'

And without waiting for a reply, Clara took the cake stand out of Mary's hands and placed it high up on top of the fridge behind her, and out of reach.

Mary wanted the cake back. Quite badly. Instead, she said, 'Thank you.'

'Owning a problem is the first step to freedom, Mary.'

Clara looked pleased. As if she'd met a new friend or, at the very least, a client.

It was time to leave. The carrot cake was way too high to get at now, and it would look undignified to jump.

As Mary hunted for her bag under the mound of tote bags

and buggies in the hall, Sandra rushed in from the garden to thrust a business card into her hand.

'Clara's very good, Mary. Especially if you and Gary ever want to ... ?'

Mary had a quick look at Clara's card. It was handmade, which might be a slight worry, but the services of a 'cut-price relationship counsellor' held particular appeal right now. Even if it had been written in glittery letters with a few typos.

Back at her own kitchen table, Mary wondered how Sandra had known her husband's name. Then she remembered she'd been screaming it quite loudly as Gary had ridden off on his motorbike.

She knew she needed help. Sometimes, Gary's insomnia could get so bad, he'd have to drive into town for a late-night takeaway, eat it in their kitchen at two in the morning, and jog round the cul-de-sac to burn off the calories.

He was as miserable as she was. It was counselling or a dog, and Gary was allergic. She'd make an appointment with Clara for a week's time, which would give her space to make a replacement curtain and possibly salvage her career.

'Do sit.' Clara waved at a wicker chair that looked as if it had just been brought in from the garden.

Mary was grateful for the additional small cushion. She didn't want the wicker to leave marks on her thighs.

Subdued sounds of a TV could be heard from the room above. This didn't feel very professional somehow. On the other hand, they both knew it wasn't Harley Street. This was cut-price counselling that had come at a good time.

'Well done for getting here.' Clara offered a small smile.

'Thank you.' Mary felt strangely pleased. Although she had navigated the two roads without much difficulty.

'I think we should put the carrot cake business behind us, Mary.'

'Okay.'

Maybe this was why Clara was cut-price. She only dealt with problems by mentioning them once.

'So how can I help you, Mary?' Clara raised her eyebrows at the same time as she posed the question.

Mary assumed this might be to help her question land with emphasis. But she wasn't sure. Maybe something else alarming had just happened that she wasn't aware of. Like a mouse running behind the wicker chair. She became distracted by a small certificate on the wall. The 'Better You' relationship counselling course had awarded Ms C. Stern a 'pass' for her foundation year. A pass seemed a bit low. Mary wished she hadn't seen it.

'Perhaps give me a bit of background?'

'Sure,' said Mary, and she began telling Clara where she was born, how her mother hadn't breast-fed her enough, and listed some of her GCSEs.

Clara raised a hand to stop her.

'Mary ...' Clara offered another small smile, possibly to temper what was to follow. 'Shall we get real?'

This was a bit harsh. Mary hadn't lied about her exams. Only one of the grades ...

'Why are you here, do you think?'

'Because you're quite local?'

Clara looked very slightly annoyed. This may have been why she only had a pass, thought Mary.

Mary knew she was stalling. She'd have to open up to Clara, but it was going to be embarrassing having to tell a stranger that her husband cried sometimes, when he couldn't get to sleep ... and that he slept on the sofa, smelling of soy sauce and garlic.

'In your own time.' Clara glanced at the clock on the wall.

'It's because I'm lonely. And because Gary and I have lost our way in our marriage. He talks over me when I begin to tell him important things, like how many people have complimented me recently about my flexible pelmet designs for small spaces, or how my cushions can light up a room using contrasting colourways. And sometimes, well ... we just don't ...'

'Make love?' Clara clasped her hands together.

'Yes, that's it.'

Mary felt relieved.

Clara nodded.

'You know what you've got, don't you, Mary?'

'No. That's why I'm here.'

'You've got ennui.'

'I don't think I have. What's ennui?'

'Ennui is a state of nothingness. Your cushions are no longer fulfilling you, which is understandable. Fabric can only go so far in connecting you to the wider universe, or even igniting the more intimate side of sensuality.'

'I still find velvet quite tactile, actually,' said Mary. Clara seemed very judgemental, even for a foundation-course counsellor.

'But shouldn't you be finding sensuality in Gary? Sandra said he's still fit.'

'How does Sandra know?' asked Mary.

This was disconcerting. She felt a bit sick.

'When they jog together.'

'I didn't know they jogged together.'

'Not far. Just enough to get puffed, she said. There's nothing in it. Sandra takes the dog with her, so they're never alone.'

Gary was now going jogging at night with her neighbour and her dog after his Horlicks. Mary felt an unpleasant surge of jealousy. How could she not have noticed? Being asleep upstairs was no excuse.

'So, here's what you do . . . I've had a lot of success with this, actually.'

'That's good. I'd like some success, please.'

'You need to go out on a date.'

'I know, that's what I keep telling him.'

'No. You need a date with someone else.'

'What about Gary?'

'Exactly. Have you thought about Sandra?'

'Why?'

'She could date Gary.'

'But . . . this is weird.'

Clara shook her head.

'This is what I do, Mary. You both have ennui and one of my specialities is connecting my co-workers with clients for ennui-prevention therapy, through co-dating.'

'But who would I date?'

'This is where Robert comes in.'

Mary looked at the ceiling nervously. Was Robert watching TV upstairs?

'Robert's my co-counselling ennui worker. Sandra's one as well. We all met on the same course, would you believe?'

Mary could believe.

'I'm sure he'd find your passion for velvet quite ... delicious?'

Clara looked almost coquettish. Mary wasn't quite sure if she felt comfortable. She preferred the raised eyebrows.

'How would this work in practice?'

'You and Robert have a date, on the same night that Gary and Sandra have a date. Then, once you've each been ignited, your ennui diminishes, and you exchange your stories.'

'We lie?'

'No, you share your feelings and reignite your love. Hey presto! End of ennui. Time's up, I'm afraid, Mary. Robert will text you. I think we said cash on the phone, didn't we?'

'We did.' Mary thrust some cash under her cushion. There didn't seem an obvious place to put it, apart from the fruit bowl where the bananas had begun to seep a little.

'Thank you, Mary. Oh, and dress up a bit, maybe?'

*

Robert was already seated when Mary rustled into her local Italian restaurant. The net underskirt had been a last-minute addition, so it was a relief to see Robert wearing a suit. There was a carnation on the table, which looked promising. Then she noticed there was a carnation on the table next to theirs as well. And on all the other tables.

Robert stood up and pulled out a chair for her. He was tall, with soft features and curly brown hair. Not unlike a male model. Had he been forty years younger. He then waited for her to be seated before he sat down himself. For one awful moment Mary wondered if Clara had booked her in with a robot. His manners seemed so finely programmed.

'Clara didn't tell me you're a fan of the opera.' He gave an appreciative smile in the direction of Mary's layering of net.

'That's because I'm not, probably.'

Robert wasn't put off. 'Or the fact that you have a glorious head of hair.'

Mary realized that paying compliments must be part of Robert's job as co-worker of Clara's ennui-prevention therapy, but she wanted to get to know Robert a bit more as a person as well. She'd be paying for it, after all.

After a bottle of wine, Mary discovered that Robert knew several cushion designers who had travelled to India to buy silk samples for bedspreads ... or so he said. Maybe he was fibbing, it didn't matter.

By the end of the evening, they had become quite passionate about the gap in the market for online curtains with pelmets. There was so much to say and so little time to say it.

They were the last in the restaurant. Mary picked up the bill.

'Let me,' Robert said, looking into her eyes, and nodding his head gently.

'No, this is part of the deal.' Mary's heart was racing.

'This isn't.' Robert leant across the table and took Mary's face in his hands. She couldn't remember when Gary had ever done that. Perhaps because they never sat opposite each other for supper. Only side by side with a tray in front of the TV.

Mary began to feel similar feelings to those she experienced when she'd dipped her finger into the cake frosting and couldn't stop.

She moved her face closer ...

After a taxi ride home involving a rather intense fantasy about how Robert might look on a sun lounger, Mary checked herself in the hall mirror. She looked flushed. She found Gary sitting on their sofa with a glass of wine in his hand. He'd used hair gel, which was a surprise.

'So, how did yours go?' she asked.

Gary's slightly spruced hair was definitely an improvement.

'Good. You?' Gary looked at her with a mix of concern and curiosity.

'Good. Why's your tie on the table?'

Gary grabbed his tie and put it into his pocket.

'Not comfy wearing it.'

'So ...' Should she tell Gary that she'd just had a curtain

epiphany with Robert? She decided against it when she heard the downstairs loo flushing.

'Who's that?'

'Only Sandra.'

Mary felt cheated. She thought of Robert and their final lingering kiss as he ran to catch his tube. What was going on? Why was she feeling so ... so *alert* all of a sudden?

'I thought you were having a date at the Chinese?'

Sandra popped her head round the door and waved a lipstick at them. She was smiling a little too brightly. And why were her two top buttons undone?

'I knew my lipstick was here somewhere, Mary! Must have dropped it when I popped in, quickly, to use the loo. I'll see myself out.'

Mary wasn't convinced. Sandra looked too dishevelled to be concerned about a missing lipstick.

Had Sandra overstepped her mark as an ennui-prevention co-worker? Why was Mary feeling so enraged about Sandra and yet so excited to see Gary?

She'd forgotten what Gary looked like out of running shorts and in long trousers. He looked good. Too good for Sandra.

As soon as the front door closed, Gary let out a sigh of relief. 'Thank God you came back.'

She noticed him look at her with an intensity she hadn't seen for a long time. 'Why? What would have happened?'

Gary slowly got up from the sofa and walked towards her. 'I've been thinking about you. For the past hour.'

'You haven't answered the question.'

But she allowed herself to be pulled towards him. She didn't care what Sandra had or hadn't done with her lipstick. She didn't care if Robert liked her hair. What mattered was the feeling of Gary's heart beating fast against her chest. And a feeling of real happiness.

'Do you think Clara's fully qualified?' asked Mary suddenly.

'In what?'

'Ennui-prevention therapy?'

'Does it matter?' said Gary.

And, for the first time in a long time, Gary went upstairs at the same time as Mary, to sleep in the marital bed . . .

Helen Lederer began her career in stand-up comedy at London's famous Comedy Store. On TV, Helen is possibly best known for her role as Catriona in *Absolutely Fabulous*. Her most recent show, 'I Might As Well Say It', was written and performed at the Edinburgh Fringe in 2018 – the same year she launched the 'Comedy Women In Print' prize. CWIP is the UK and Ireland's first comedic literary prize to celebrate witty women authors.

Her published books include *Coping with Helen Lederer* (Angus & Robertson), *Single Minding* (Hodder & Stoughton) and *Finger Food* (Accent Press). Her comedy novel *Losing It* (Pan Macmillan) was nominated for the Bollinger Everyman Wodehouse Prize in 2015. Helen has written and starred in two series of *Life with Lederer* and *All Change* for BBC Radio 4. She's agony aunt for *My Weekly* magazine and currently writes for the *Daily Telegraph* and *The Times*.

A Relaxing Day of Retail Therapy

by Rachel Hore

'I t'll take your mind off things.' Janet's voice sounded so definite down the phone.

'I don't feel like shopping.' Gemma screwed up her tired eyes. 'Besides, I've no money.'

'We can at least look.'

'I don't feel like looking. Or even leaving the house.'

'Gemma, you can't stay in forever.'

'But what if I'm recognized?'

'It was the *Eastern Gazette*, not Sky News. Cat litter by now.'

The thought of her photograph lying under a feline bottom did not reassure Gemma.

'I must say though,' she sighed, 'I am getting cabin fever. All right. I'll meet you at the bus stop in half an hour.'

'You've had a hard few months,' Janet told her as they stepped down from the bus by the entrance to Chapelwood Mall. 'A relaxing day of retail therapy is just what you need. And I'll treat you to lunch in Samsons.'

Gemma liked Samsons, but she liked the Butternut Café

better. She opened her mouth to say so, but Janet was already sweeping through the automatic doors into the mall, a glass and silver wonder palace redolent with the scent of candyfloss and donuts from the Chocolate Sprinkles bakery.

'Woohoo,' Janet cried, with the vigour of a warhorse at the sound of a bugle. 'Where shall we start?'

'Marks and Spencer?' Gemma said weakly. She usually bought her clothes there, click and collect. They did a short length in trousers and she could try things on at home.

'I think John Lewis,' Janet said, and marched off towards the bright white lights of the store at the far end of the hall.

'Janet . . .' Gemma called after her. 'Dammit.' She set off in pursuit.

Gemma was very fond of Janet. They'd met at the school gate when their daughters were five and still under their mothers' thumbs for playdates and birthday parties. She'd liked Janet's can-do attitude and the way she challenged the punitive uniform rules. Gemma was gentler and hated conflict, but then Janet often said she wished she had Gemma's quiet gift of listening to people.

Their daughters' interests diverged and as teenagers they drifted apart. Gemma and Janet continued to be close, though the girls rolled their eyes at any attempts to resurrect the childhood friendship. They weren't even girls any more, but young women with jobs and life partners.

That fluffy jumper would really suit Natalie, Gemma thought as they passed the own-brand sale rack, but Janet was going too fast to allow her to look.

'Coast,' Janet said, stopping at a rail of black trousers and tops. She picked out a sparkly shirt. 'Try this,' she said, thrusting it at Gemma, 'and a size up.' Another joined it. 'And these trousers are nice.'

'I'm not sure they're me ...' Gemma began.

Janet narrowed her thick-lashed eyes. 'We're wanting a new you. Won't you give them a go?'

Gemma sighed, but she trusted her friend's taste. Janet, tall and of cuddly proportions, always drew admiring glances for the simple lines and strong patterns of her tunics and dresses.

A lanky salesman shimmied up. Gemma felt panic rise at his beady-eyed stare, but all he said was, 'Would we like to try these on?'

'We would. Wait ...' Janet gathered a green dress with a scoop neckline, then a flamingo-pink blouse decorated with tiny palm trees.

In the privacy of the changing room Gemma sank on to a plush stool, but Janet was in the next cubicle trying on a gorgeous blue and red checked tunic and she knew she'd better get on with it. Reluctantly, she began to undress.

Janet, she had to admit, had a good eye. The trousers slid easily on to her short square figure, slimming the hips, and the palm-tree blouse finished at the right length. The only trouble was, it wasn't the Gemma she knew who looked back at her from the mirror.

But since the awful thing in the newspaper she didn't know who that Gemma was any more.

She eyed her reflection for a while, twisting and turning. The tag was digging into the back of her neck and she pulled it up and squinted at the price. Her eyes widened. Whoever this new Gemma might be she still couldn't afford clothes like this! She stripped and was about to pull her comfortable jeans and sweater back on when her gaze fell on the green dress. It was undoubtedly pretty.

'Gemma?' Janet's voice beyond the curtain made her flinch.

'Wait a moment.' Hastily Gemma unhooked the dress from its hanger then pulled it over her head. Some concerted wriggling and it was done. She stared at herself, bug-eyed. Sparkling hazel eyes, creamy shoulders rising from a ruff of pale green that brought out the fair lights in her mid-brown hair, the knee-length skirt flaring flatteringly ... but she'd never worn anything with such a low neck. She couldn't, she'd be so aware of herself, worried that she'd fall out.

'Are you decent?' Janet sang.

'Just about,' Gemma breathed as Janet twitched the curtain aside.

'Oh, *darling*, you look gorgeous. Let's just ...' Janet pulled and prodded until the dress hung to her satisfaction. 'Wait till Brian sees you in this, girl. He'll regret everything.'

Gemma's shoulders slumped. Was this what things had come to, dressing up to lure back her indifferent mate? It wasn't her boobs she needed Brian to love. 'It's far too expensive,' she whispered. Oh, the relief when Janet withdrew and she could wrap herself in her familiar clothes again.

Outside she waited while Janet paid for the tunic and a pair of velvet jeggings. A part-time teaching assistant, Gemma was a little envious of what Janet, a marketing executive, could afford. She watched her friend examine several credit cards before sliding one into the machine.

'Phew,' Janet said, as the payment went through. She collected her plastic carrier bag. 'Time for coffee?'

Gemma's cappuccino was rich and creamy, and the blueberry muffin meltingly delicious. On the minus side she was shocked when Janet was sharp with the waitress who forgot the oat milk for her Americano. Her friend could be tactless, but never rude.

As she sipped her foamy coffee she remembered the beady-eyed sales assistant. 'He looked at me strangely. Do you think he recognized me from the paper?'

'No.' Janet frowned. 'I hope you're not getting paranoid.'

'Oh, thanks for that!'

'I'm sorry.' Janet flashed one of her generous smiles, a glimpse of her usual self.

'I'm thinking about that green dress,' Gemma said in concession. 'But Brian would be furious at the expense.'

'Not once he saw you in it.'

Gemma made a face and changed the subject. 'Where next?'

'Cosmetics, I think. War paint always works marvels.'

Gemma had to admit that she loved the beauty hall with its coruscating light, the breath of perfume in the air and the neat little pots of dreams in sleek white and gold packaging. Janet bought an eye-shadow palette and her favourite Jo Malone bath oil. She used yet another credit card.

'Wait.' On the way out of the shop Gemma paused at the sale rack. The fluffy jumper was the right size. Twenty quid, and her daughter would love it. She bore it to the sales desk where the same assistant looked at her shrewdly. 'If you don't mind me asking, aren't you—?'

'No, I'm not,' she said firmly, and handed him two ten-pound notes.

The rest of the morning was exhausting. Two boutiques, one dark with thudding music and odd clothes with unexpected holes and ragged hems, the other full of bright colours, the air cloudy with incense. Janet bought a floaty red dress in Indian cotton and a long string of beads. Gemma chose a cheap macramé keyring to show willing. In Marks & Spencer she offered her opinion as Janet paraded in a succession of outfits. But when her friend paid for a cape and a pair of boots Gemma watched, horrified, as Janet's first three credit cards were rejected.

'Is everything OK?' she whispered, but her friend snapped back.

'It's fine. Now, lunch, don't you think?'

Samsons (Gemma, with her teaching hat on, always thought it should have an apostrophe) was a tiled cave with glass-topped tables and a bar. A lad with a white apron and a nose ring showed them to a table. Nearby a couple of hefty young men in suits sat scrolling on their phones as they drank foaming pints of beer.

'This is on me,' Janet reminded her firmly.

'Honestly, you don't need to,' Gemma stuttered in dismay, but Janet was already ordering glasses of wine and a lobster salad.

The Butternut Café was homespun and she'd have felt more comfortable there. Besides, the waiter was looking at her curiously and she remembered that she was wearing the same striped scarf as in the newspaper. She unwound it and stuffed it into her handbag as she asked for an inexpensive risotto.

The wine was delicious but it made her muzzy and it loosened Janet's tongue. She talked nonstop in a way that was almost manic. About an expensive coat she'd ordered online and the new kitchen she was planning.

It wasn't fair, Gemma thought, as she toyed with buttery rice and mushroom. Janet knew how little she and Brian had to live on, but she was throwing her wealth in Gemma's face.

The final straw came as the waiter was preparing the bill.

The men on the nearby table were leaving. 'Excuse us, lady,' one said to Gemma. He showed her his phone. 'This is you, innit?'

Gemma stared at the screen, her mouth frozen open in the same big O of horror she wore in the photograph. There she was in all her glory, clambering out of the car she'd just rolled on top of a grassy roundabout. She'd been so distracted she'd had to swerve wildly to avoid her Fiat being crushed by a lorry.

She pushed the phone away. The man was roaring with laughter. 'Me and my mate here,' he said. 'Funniest thing ever. You must have felt well stupid.'

The men crept away. Janet started to giggle. 'Sorry, Gemma, but you have to admit—'

Something snapped in Gemma's head.

'No, it wasn't funny,' she shouted. 'It was horrible and frightening and I'll be charged for careless driving.'

Janet laughed louder. 'I can't help it.'

'And I'm fed up with today. Why do you never listen to me? All this stuff you've bought and it was supposed to be my day out. And you know I don't have much money.'

'I said I'd pay for the meal.' Janet looked panicked.

'That's what I mean. All you've done is splash cash. It's as though you're taunting me.'

'I didn't mean—'

'You may not have meant it, but that's what it feels like.' Now she'd started it was difficult to stop. All the anguish of the last few months poured out.

'And something's wrong with you and you're not telling me. Why do you have all those credit cards that don't work?'

Tough Janet sagged like a deflating balloon. There were tears in her eyes. The shock pulled Gemma up short.

'Jan? What is it you're not telling me?'

'I . . . I'm sorry. Sorry for everything you've said. You must think . . . the clothes, the new kitchen. The thing is, Gemma, I can't stop myself. What shall I do? I can't pay for it all.'

'Are you serious?'

'Yes, completely.' She took out another credit card. 'This is my last one,' she said, tossing it on the dish with the bill. 'And I'm crossing my fingers it'll work.'

'No,' Gemma said firmly, pulling out her purse. 'Stuff Brian. I'm paying for this. And listen, Janet. This afternoon we're going back round all the shops to take back what you've bought. I mean it.'

'I can't. I'd be too embarrassed.'

'Then I'll do the talking. After making a fool of myself on that roundabout nothing is embarrassing any more. Never mind my problems. We're going to sort *you* out.'

Janet stared at her, an expression of admiration in her eyes that Gemma had never seen before.

'And then,' she said, her heart swelling with pleasure, 'we're going back to John Lewis. I've decided to buy that green dress.'

Rachel Hore worked in London publishing for many years before moving with her family to Norwich. She taught publishing and creative writing at the University of East Anglia before becoming a full-time writer. Many of her eleven novels have been *Sunday Times* top-ten bestsellers. *A Gathering Storm* and *Last Letter Home* were each chosen for Richard & Judy's Book Club. Her latest bestseller is *The Love Child* and a new novel, *A Beautiful Spy*, has recently been published by Simon & Schuster. Rachel studied history at university and enjoys reading and writing historical fiction.

Copyrights and Credits